CHARMING A TEXAS BEAST

Copyright © 2022 by Katie Lane

Printed in the USA.

Cover Design and Interior Format
© KILLION
THE
GROUP INC.

# Charming a

# TEXAS BEAST

**KINGMAN RANCH**
**·1·**

# KATIE LANE

*To Lori Tillery, the best bestie ever*

# CHAPTER ONE

T HE TOWN OF CURSED, TEXAS, came by its name honestly.

Droughts, pestilence, dust storms, floods, tornados, Indians, and outlaws beset the first settlers. That was just in the first year. A large percentage of the pioneers gave up and moved on, hoping to find a more welcoming place to settle. Only the hardest, toughest, and most stubborn folks stayed. Honest folks who believed in calling a spade a spade. They weren't about to call their unlucky town Blessed.

Over the years, things didn't get much better. It became a badge of honor to live in Cursed. The townsfolk were quite proud of being the type of people who could survive anything.

Not only survive but thrive.

Although as Lillian Leigh Daltry drove through Cursed, it didn't look like her hometown was thriving. The old gas station had only one working pump. The restaurant was in a crumbling building with a faded sign on one wall that said Good Eats. And Nasty Jack's bar still had no sign at all, blacked out windows, and a hitching post

in front. Even with the storm brewing overhead, there were three horses tied to the hitching
post—and more than a dozen dusty trucks parked
in the lot.

The post office, feed store, and small grocery
store weren't as run-down, but they were in need
of renovations. Only the business at the end of
the main street looked prosperous. The rambling
farmhouse was painted a pristine white with
pretty navy-blue shutters and a bright red door.
In the living room window a neon sign hung:
*Fortunetelling and Palm Reading.* In a town that was
cursed, fortunetellers and palm readers were an
absolute must.

As was a church.

Holy Gossip with its sky-high bell tower was
the biggest building in town.

Just not the biggest building in the county.

Kingman Ranch held that honor. While the
town was cursed, the Kingmans had been more
than blessed. They owned one of the biggest
ranches in Texas and had built a castle to prove
it. The townsfolk of Cursed referred to the huge
mansion in many different ways: Bucking-Horse
Palace. Kingman's Folly. Western Camelot. Cowboy Castle. And One Big-Assed House. But Lily
had always thought of the massive house with its
multiple turrets in only one way.

Home.

Not that Lily had ever lived in the sprawling
stone structure with its cultured marble bath-
rooms, dining room table that could seat half
the congregation of Holy Gossip, and its base-

ment with the bar bigger than the one at Nasty Jack's. But she had lived in the gardener's cottage just a short distance from the main house. She'd lived there with her loving parents, who'd been the Kingmans' gardeners until her mother passed away. Then she'd lived there with her father . . . until she'd turned eighteen and completely humiliated herself.

Lily's face still heated with embarrassment every time she thought of that night. But she wasn't a naïve teenager anymore. She was a successful, mature woman who was no longer starstruck by a handsome prince cowboy who lived in a Texas castle.

Which didn't explain why her heart added an extra beat and her sweaty hands clenched the steering wheel of the rental car as she turned off the highway and drove under the stone entrance to the Kingman Ranch with its two sculpted rearing stallions. When she rounded a bend and the castle came into view, her anxiety increased tenfold.

The mansion didn't look like a fairytale castle tonight. Angry, black clouds completely obliterated the moon and stars. The pitch-black night, lit only by the occasional bolt of jagged lightning, made the house look less like Cinderella's castle and more like Dr. Frankenstein's. It had yet to rain. But Lily knew the skies were only moments away from releasing a torrent, so she wasted no time driving over the pond bridge and circling around the large house to the cottage in back.

While the Kingman house was big and grand,

the cottage was small and quaint. Her mother had designed the river rock house and it looked like it belonged in the English countryside rather than on a Texas ranch. The roof was steep and shingled with cedar and the windows were multi-paned with brightly painted boxes beneath that held a flourish of spring flowers.

Grief consumed Lily at just the sight of her beloved home. Or maybe what caused her grief was that Gwen Daltry was no longer inside to greet her with a tight hug and warm English biscuits straight from the oven. She was no longer there to tenderly brush Lily's hair and tell her she was the most talented, beautiful girl in the world. She was no longer there to hear about her daughter's greatest accomplishments . . . or her worst fears.

While Lily loved her father, they had never had the close connection she and her mother had. Theodore Daltry was a quiet man who kept his thoughts to himself. Similar to Lily. Gwen had been the outgoing and gregarious one in the family. The one who made every day sparkle. With her gone, the cottage had lost all its life. Now it was just a place Lily had once lived.

A boom of thunder split the night, startling her out of her thoughts. She quickly pulled next to the cottage and got out. Since it was so late, she didn't expect her father to be waiting up—especially when he was on painkillers for his broken leg. But she had expected him to leave a light on and the door unlocked. The cottage was dark, and both the front and back doors were bolted tight. Which was odd. The doors had never been locked when she'd lived there. There was no need. Everyone who worked on the ranch was trusted.

She knocked on the door. "Daddy? It's Lily."

When her father didn't answer, she began to grow concerned. She grew even more concerned when she called his cell phone and it went straight to voice mail. Another clap of thunder had her jumping. A second later the skies opened, and rain poured down. She had wanted to avoid the Kingman family as much as possible while taking care of her father, but now she had no choice. They would know where her father was or have a key to the cottage. Hopefully, her father wasn't inside and unable to answer the door or phone.

With rain pummeling her, she hurried along the brick path that led to the back door of the Kingman castle. One of her spiked heels got caught in a crack between bricks and she went down hard, ripping her dress and scraping one knee. By the time she reached the door, she was a hot mess. So much for returning home looking like a mature, successful woman. But worry for her father overrode her ego, and she pounded on the sturdy oak door with its bronze Texas star. When minutes passed and no one answered, she tried the doorknob. Thankfully, it was unlocked.

As a child, she'd been scared to enter the house at night. The high, echoing ceilings and long, dark hallways had her imagination running wild with images of ghosts and ghouls. Now, the only fear she had was for her father.

"Hello?" she called as she stepped into the

mudroom. "Anyone home?"

She flipped the light switch, but nothing happened. The flashlight on her phone didn't work either. She couldn't even get the screen to come up. She'd obviously broken it when she fell. She placed the phone on a bench by the door and moved into the dark kitchen. A flickering light drew her across the grand foyer into the main living area.

A fire burned low in the massive floor-to-ceiling Austin stone fireplace. No one seemed to be enjoying the deep orange glow of the dying embers, but it looked as if someone had been. A half glass of amber liquid and an open book sat on a table next to a huge chair made of cowhide leather.

The Kingman throne.

The patriarch of the Kingman family, Charlie Kingman, or King as he'd been called, had sat in that very chair while presiding over family gatherings. Lily had been too little to remember much about the man. All she remembered was that he'd been big, mean, and bossy. After he'd passed away, his son, Douglas, had presided over the ranch. But Douglas had never sat in the chair. Maybe because he'd been a much smaller, nicer man who had felt uncomfortable sitting in the pretentious piece of furniture.

But when he passed away, his son Stetson had no problem taking over the Kingman throne. Or filling his grandfather's boots. Stetson was just as much of an arrogant beast as his grandfather had been. And just another reason Lily had stayed away from the ranch until now.

Turning from the fire, she headed down the hallway to the grand staircase that led to the bedrooms. She hated to wake the entire house, but she was willing to do whatever it took to find her father.

As she climbed the curved marble stairs, a chill of remembrance ran through her. She had followed the same path on her high school graduation night. But she hadn't been looking for her father that night. She'd been looking for Stetson's brother Wolfe Kingman, the boy who had starred in all her fantasies since she was old enough to feel the first stirrings of sexual awareness. Wolfe, whose handsome face made her heart beat faster and her knees turn to water. Wolfe, who always had a wink and a smile to give the gardener's shy daughter.

The soft click of boot heels on marble stairs startled her out of her thoughts. She whirled and the wet soles of her shoes slipped. She might have plummeted to her death if she hadn't been stopped by what felt like a solid brick wall.

But the arms that encircled her weren't made of brick. They were made of hard muscle and warm skin. They easily caught her and lifted her against an even harder chest. It was too dark to see his face. But she didn't need to. Her body had only reacted this way to one man.

Wolfe.

Anger that a man she hadn't seen in close to eight years could make her heart flutter and her pulse race had her stiffening in his arms and speaking sharply. "Put me down."

He didn't answer. His arms tightened and he carried her down the stairs as she tried not to notice the flex of his muscles and the warmth of his bare skin. When they reached the bottom, she expected him to set her on her feet. Instead, he carried her into the living room and placed her in King's chair.

When he stepped back, she drew in a sharp breath. He wasn't the prince charming she expected.

He was the beast.

Stetson.

The shadows cast by the dying embers emphasized the hard angles of his face, his deep-set eyes, and the faint white scars that covered his left cheek. Lily didn't know how the oldest Kingman had gotten the scars and she'd always been too terrified of Stetson to ask.

And with due cause.

"What the hell are you doing sneaking around in the dark?" he growled. "If you had fallen down those stairs, you could've broken your fool neck."

When she was little, she'd always burst into tears and run away whenever Stetson got after her. But she was no longer a scared little girl . . . at least, that's what she kept telling herself.

She stiffened her spine and met his hard gaze head on. "I wouldn't have startled and almost fallen if you hadn't snuck up behind me. And I wasn't sneaking around in your house. I knocked on the door, but no one answered."

"So you just came right in?"

"Your father made sure everyone knew they could always come right in. Obviously, you don't put out the same welcome mat."

Stetson leaned closer, the glowing embers reflecting in his polished onyx eyes. "Sometimes it's not a good idea to walk into people's houses without an invitation, Goldilocks. I thought you would've learned that the night you tried to sneak into Wolfe's bed."

Her face flamed with embarrassment. She had hoped Stetson would have forgotten that night. She should've known better. He wasn't the type of man who forgot things . . . or let them go.

She pushed down her humiliation and got to the reason for her visit. "I'm looking for my father. I went to the cottage, but the doors are locked and he wouldn't answer my knock or the phone."

"Because he's here. When the power went out, I thought he'd be safer in the guest room."

Her shoulders relaxed and she leaned her head back against the chair and closed her eyes. "Thank God. I worried he was lying inside the cottage unable to move or wandering around in this storm delusional from the pain medication the doctor gave him." A snort had her eyes flashing open. Even in the low light, it was easy to read the contempt on Stetson's face.

"You were worried? Since when do you care about your father, Lillian Leigh?"

Disbelief and anger had her sitting straight up. "Excuse me?"

He cocked his head and stared down at her.

Had he gotten even taller and more muscular or was it just a trick of the shadows from the glowing firelight? "Do I have it wrong? Have you been secretly visiting your daddy and I wasn't aware of it? Because I haven't seen you anywhere around for the last eight years. You weren't here when he caught the flu and was in bed for a week. You weren't here when he cut his hand sharpening his hedge trimmers and had to have twelve stitches. You weren't here when he fell off a ladder and broke his leg in two places. And you sure haven't been here for any holidays, birthdays, or your mother's birthdays and the anniversary of her death when your father takes flowers to her grave . . . alone."

Lily hadn't known about her father's illness or his accident with the hedge trimmers. Both upset her. But what caused a hard lump of emotion to form in her throat was the thought of him going to her mother's grave site. Alone.

"And yet all he does is brag about you," Stetson continued. "He bursts with pride every time he shows me a book you just released or a children's writers' award you won."

Her father was proud of her? Why had he never told her? Probably the same reason he hadn't told her about his accidents, illnesses, and visits to the cemetery. She wouldn't have known that he broke his leg if the doctor hadn't called her because she was listed as his next of kin. And yet, it seemed he had no trouble talking to Stetson. That hurt. It hurt a lot. But Stetson had always known exactly what to say to hurt her.

He wasn't done yet.

"What makes absolutely no sense to me is that you have all the time in the world for your writing, but you can't make time to come see your own father. In my book, that's nothing but selfishness."

She wanted to argue, but the truth of Stetson's words cut right through her. Tears of guilt filled her eyes. She tried to blink them away. When she couldn't, she jumped up and headed for the door.

It seemed that things at the Kingman Ranch hadn't changed after all.

Stetson could still make her cry.

# CHAPTER TWO

STETSON DIDN'T KNOW WHY HE stood there feeling like the biggest bully in all of Texas. He had nothing to feel guilty about. He'd only told the truth. Lily *had* neglected her father. Theodore Daltry was a good man who had always been there for the entire Kingman family—especially Stetson. After Stetson's father died and left him in charge of the ranch, it was Theo who had offered a listening ear and sound advice. Stetson trusted him. Not only as a dependable employee, but also as a loyal friend. It ticked him off that Theo's own daughter didn't seem to care about her father at all.

As Stetson had always thought, Lily was just like her mama.

Unfortunately, Theo hadn't seen any fault in his wife. And he certainly didn't see any in his daughter. He would be thoroughly disappointed in Stetson if he found out he had made Lily cry and sent her out in a monsoon.

"Damn." Stetson blew out his breath and headed after her.

But Lily had always been a fast little thing. As

a kid, she'd been like a hummingbird—fluttering around one second and gone the next. When he reached the kitchen, the back door was already slamming closed. He cussed a blue streak as he grabbed a rain poncho and his cowboy hat from the hooks. He pulled them on, and then grabbed another slicker before heading out.

The storm had grown worse. Through the needle-sharp rain, he could barely make out Lily's white dress in front of him. Who wore white to a ranch? And sky-high heels you could break your fool neck in? Obviously, Lily had become a hoity-toity metropolitan woman who didn't belong in the country. In fact, she'd never belonged here. She was too quiet and fragile for ranch life.

He remembered the day she'd shown up at the ranch with the English couple his grandfather had hired to build a garden that would rival any garden in the world. Lily had been no more than four. A tiny thing with big green eyes that had stared right through Stetson. He'd thought she was cute and had smiled at her. She'd hidden behind her mother and started to cry. Since Stetson had just been tossed off his horse into a mesquite tree and had twenty-six stitches criss-crossing his cheek, he'd understood why. He'd spent the next year trying to get her to realize that he wasn't a scary monster. But after the night of his mother's death, he hadn't cared if Lily liked him. He still didn't.

He tugged his hat lower and caught up with her. "Would you just hold your horses?" he yelled as he grabbed her arm and pulled her to a stop.

She jerked away. In the house, her voice had been prissy with only a hint of a Texas accent. Now that she was madder than a wet hen, her twang was as thick as the raindrops. "Don't yew dare say that I don't care about my daddy! I talk to him every week and have offered him more than a few plane tickets to come see me. I'm sure he hasn't taken them because his demanding boss won't let him off work."

"Oh, so now I'm the one keeping you from your daddy," he fired back. "Don't use me as your scapegoat. If Theo wants to fly out to see you, he can go anytime and he knows it. But he hates traveling on airplanes. Something you'd know if you weren't so self-centered." He flung the poncho over her, then tugged the ends until her head popped out. He expected more sass, but when she spoke her voice was soft and strained.

"Daddy is afraid to fly?"

Stetson rolled his eyes. How clueless could a daughter be? But he wasn't about to take it up with her in the middle of a toad-choking storm.

"Come on. Let's get inside before we're both struck by lightning." He placed a hand on her back and steered her through the pelting rain to the cottage.

Her petite size had always made him feel like an awkward giant, and that hadn't changed. Even in high heels, her head barely reached his shoulders. Beneath his hand, he felt a shiver run through her and quickly pushed back his poncho and took the cottage key from his jeans pocket.

He had always loved the little stone cottage. It had seemed like more of a home than the huge monstrosity his grandfather had built. King had thought that bigger was better. Stetson had learned that bigger was only more. More work. More responsibility. More trouble.

Once he got Lily inside, he headed to her car to get her luggage. His temper had started to cool. But when he found the small carry-on in the trunk of the rental sedan, he got angry all over again. Her father had broken his leg and she only planned on staying a few days? He grabbed the bag and stomped back to the cottage. But before he could let her have it, the lights came on, and he got his first real look at how Lillian Leigh Daltry had filled out in the last eight years.

She'd filled out nicely.

She was soaked to the skin. The wet knit of her dress clung to the swells of her full breasts and the curves of her shapely hips. Suddenly, Stetson's mouth felt extremely dry. His gaze lowered to the split seam of her dress. She might be a little thing, but she had nice legs. Stetson couldn't stop his gaze from running the toned length from high thigh to trim ankle. It halted when he noticed the blood on her knee.

"You're hurt?"

She glanced down. "It's nothing. Just a scrape."

He should've let it go. But damned if he could. He set the suitcase down and moved into the living room to kneel in front of her. She jumped like a startled doe when he placed his hand on the back of her knee. His insides startled too at the feel of her warm, smooth skin beneath his cold fingers.

He cleared his throat and released her leg. "You're right. It's just a scrape." He stood and found her looking at him with big green eyes. Eyes the exact color of her mother's. Stetson couldn't help wondering how many men those eyes had pulled into their swirling depths.

He wouldn't be one of them.

He turned to the door. "I'll let your father know you're here when he wakes."

"Stetson."

He turned around.

"Thank you," she said in a soft voice. "Thank you for being here for my daddy." She swallowed hard. "Especially when I wasn't. You're right. I'm a horrible daughter. I should've come back sooner. It's just that he acted like everything was fine. Because he's always been so capable and strong, I believed him."

"Your father is capable and strong, Lily. But even capable, strong people need to be taken care of once in a while." He glanced down at the suitcase. "For more than just a random weekend. Now get out of those wet clothes before you catch pneumonia."

"You can't catch pneumonia from wet clothes."

He shrugged. "Then leave them on, but lock the door after I go."

She looked confused. "Since when do we lock doors at the ranch?"

Since the barn fire and mutilated bull. But Stetson didn't say that. "What can I say? I've become overly cautious in my old age."

"And yet you don't lock your doors."

"An oversight." More like an invitation. He would love for the animal mutilator and arsonist to come into his lair so he could beat the sonofa-bitch within an inch of his life.

Lily studied him as if reading his mind. "You never overlook things, Stetson."

She was right. But occasionally you needed to overlook things . . . like how a wet dress clung to a woman's body. And how that body had felt in his arms.

"Goodnight, Lily." He opened the door and stepped out into the storm.

As he made his way back to the house, he noticed the light in the south tower. When he got inside, he toed off his wet cowboy boots and quickly took off his poncho and hat. Two long flights of stairs later, he reached his oldest sister's room. He tapped lightly before he opened the door and peeked in.

Adeline stood in the open doors that led to the balcony, looking out at the storm. Wind whipped her pale blond hair and her nightgown around her, giving her the look of some wild siren.

She had gotten their mother's beauty. Few men could talk to Adeline without getting tongue-tied or falling head over heels in love. But she'd had only one love in her life. Sadly, Danny had been killed in Iraq nine months earlier. Stetson worried that his sister would just as soon die too than go on living without him. Sometimes, when Stetson looked into her vacant blue eyes, he wondered if she hadn't already died. There didn't seem to be a glimmer left of the laughing, loving sister he'd grown up with.

"You okay, Addie?" he asked as he stepped into the room.

She brushed at her cheeks. Whether it was rain or tears he didn't know. She closed the balcony doors before she turned to him with a smile so forced it broke his heart. "Hey, Stet. What are you doing up so late?"

"I could ask you the same."

She shrugged. "I just couldn't sleep."

He started to give her another lecture about accepting Danny's death and moving on, but he was too tired tonight to make the effort. Besides, his lectures didn't seem to be working. He moved into the room and flopped down on the bed, stuffing one of the pillows beneath his head.

"Lily Daltry came home."

His sister looked surprised. "I didn't think she'd ever come back to the States."

"She's only staying for a few days. Although that might be for the best. Wolfe's at the stock show this weekend, and he doesn't need to see how she's grown up."

Adeline's eyebrows lifted. "I guess Lily grew into a woman as beautiful as her mother."

"More so." Addie's *hmm* had Stetson glancing at her. "Just an observation. I'm not interested in Lily Daltry. Not only is she not my type, she's just a kid."

"She's a year younger than Wolfe. Twenty-six isn't a kid."

"It is to me." He ran a hand over his face. "Sometimes I feel like I'm sixty instead of thirty-one." He felt the mattress sag and lowered his hand to see Adeline sitting there. Had she lost more weight? She seemed thinner. And paler. But her eyes held the unconditional love that had always soothed Stetson's soul.

"I'm sorry, Stet. I'm sorry you had to take over running the ranch at such an early age. I know it's been a huge burden."

He was sorry too. He would've loved to finish college and just be a carefree young man like Wolfe and Buck. But as the oldest, the responsibility of running the huge Kingman Ranch had fallen to him. As did the responsibility of his family. And Adeline had enough to worry about without worrying about him.

He took her hand and squeezed it. "I love the ranch and always planned to take over when Daddy passed. It's okay I got the reins sooner than expected. It's just that lately . . . things have been a little hectic."

Adeline hesitated before she replied. "Maybe we should've reported the fire and the mutilation to the county sheriff."

Stetson released her hand and sat up. "You know what happens on the ranch stays on the ranch, Addie."

"That's Grandpa talking. Sometimes you need to call in help."

He shook his head. "Sheriff Dobbs and Deputy Tater are two of the most incompetent law officers in Texas. They couldn't find their butts with both hands. I'll handle it."

Adeline sighed and got up from the bed. "Of course you will. You seem to want to handle everything. Which is why you feel so old."

She had a good point, but he had no choice. As the oldest, he had a responsibility to keep his family and the ranch safe. And he would. Come hell or high water. Or barn fires and mutilations.

He got to his feet. "I'm going to bed, and you should too."

"I wish it was that easy."

He knew she hadn't slept much since Danny's passing. "Maybe you should take one of the pills the doc gave you after . . ." He let the sentence drift off.

She nodded. "Maybe I will."

A thought struck him. "Just one, right?"

She smiled sadly. "I'm not going to kill myself, Stetson."

"I know," he lied. "I just don't want you sleeping the day away tomorrow. I count on you. Have you had any luck finding a new housekeeper?"

"Unfortunately, no."

He shook his head. "I should give the job of finding one to Wolfe and Buck. We wouldn't need a new housekeeper if they hadn't gotten into a wrestling match and scared the last one away."

"It wasn't Wolfe and Buck who scared Carmel away." She sent him a pointed look.

Stetson stared at her in shock. "Me? I never said more than two words to the woman."

"Sometimes a scowl speaks louder than words.

If we want to keep the next housekeeper, you need to try smiling more." He forced a smile, and she cringed. "I said smile, not bare your teeth like a mad badger waiting to pounce."

"A mad badger?" He smiled evilly and moved toward her. "I'll show you a mad badger waiting to pounce."

She backed away and held up her hands. "Don't you dare, Stetson Douglas King—" She cut off and shrieked when he tossed her on the bed, then proceeded to tickle the bottoms of her feet until she wiggled like a worm on a hook and laughed uncontrollably. He had missed that laugh.

"Stop," she gasped, "or I swear I'll—"

The door swung open and Buck came charging into the room in his underwear waving a .45 like Wild Bill Hickok. Right behind him was their youngest sister Delaney, carrying one of her high school softball bats. They both stopped short when they saw Stetson.

"Shit," Buck said. "I thought someone had gotten in the house and was attacking Addie."

Adeline sat up. "For God's sake, Buck, put that thing away before you accidentally shoot someone."

"Not likely." Buck executed a perfect gunslinger move and spun the revolver on his finger a few times before tucking it into the waistband of his boxers.

Stetson never liked anyone getting cocky with guns. "If that gun is loaded, I'm going to kick your ass."

Buck held up his hands. "Easy, big bro. I'm not

stupid."

"Really?" Delaney said. "Because only an idiot would try to save someone with an unloaded gun, little brother."

"And a bat is better? Stop calling me little brother. I'm only three minutes younger than you, Del." Buck puffed out his chest. "And I'm much bigger."

Knowing an argument was about to ensue, Stetson cut in. "There's no reason for a gun or a bat. I was just checking in on Adeline before I went to bed."

"What are you doing up so late?" Delaney asked.

Adeline answered. "Lily Daltry came back to the ranch."

"Lily's back?" Buck said. "Is she still weird?"

"She wasn't weird," Delaney snapped. "She was just shy."

"Weirdly shy. I could never get two words out of her, and I can talk to anyone."

Stetson had gotten more than two words out of her. He'd also made her cry. Once again, a feeling of guilt settled in his belly, but he ignored it and ushered his little brother and sister to the door.

"It doesn't matter if Lily is weird or not. She won't be staying long. Now we all need to get some sleep. Tomorrow will be another busy day."

But once in bed, sleep evaded Stetson. He worried about Adeline getting over her grief. He worried about Wolfe getting too rowdy in Dallas and getting his butt tossed in jail. He worried about Delaney spending too much time around rough cowboys. He worried about Buck being too cocky with his gun. He worried about the person responsible for the fire and the mutilated bull.

And he worried about Theo—which got him thinking about Theo's daughter.

When he finally did fall asleep, his dreams were filled with white lilies.

# CHAPTER THREE

JET LAG HAD LILY FALLING asleep as soon as her head hit the pillow, but she woke up in the wee hours of the morning, feeling guilty. She had thought her father was doing just fine. Every time they talked, he had acted like his life was going on as usual. He'd never mentioned getting the flu or cutting his hand . . . or taking flowers to her mother's grave. In fact, he rarely mentioned Gwen at all. Which led Lily to believe he was handling his grief much better than she was handling hers.

But she should've known better.

Like her father, she had kept all their conversations lighthearted and positive. She hadn't told him about how depressed she'd been when she'd gotten to Oxford University. Or how she'd felt like a misfit in a foreign country nothing like her Texan home. She hadn't told him about how she'd kept to herself and hidden away in her dorm room like a recluse. When he called, she'd fabricated tales of all the friends she'd made and all the things they did together.

It wasn't until she'd sold her first Fairy Prairie

story after graduating that she'd finally started to come out of her depression and feel comfortable in England. She'd moved to her mother's hometown of Shere, Surrey, where she rented a small cottage. She spent her days sketching and writing her fairy stories and her weekends reading in small cafés or riding her bike through the countryside. Occasionally, she'd go to London to meet with her editor or agent. Or travel around the UK to do readings at bookstores—children never seemed to make her feel as shy and awkward as adults did. When she'd talked to her father, she hadn't had to lie about being okay.

But it seemed he had.

She should've come back to see him. They might not be close, but he was her father. He was all the family she had left.

At dawn, she finally drifted back to sleep. She started awake what felt like only moments later to sunlight pouring across her bed and the familiar sound of her father's voice. It still held a slight English accent, but Texas country had flavored his speech.

"Now, there was no reason to bring me all the way home, Stetson. I could've managed just fine on my own."

Lily threw back the covers and jumped up. She found her father and Stetson in the living room. Her father had always been so robust and healthy. It was hard to see him sitting in a wheelchair with his leg propped up in a cast. Or to see the way age had creased his face and sprinkled his thick black hair with gray.

His kind brown eyes lit up when he saw her. "Lilliput!" He held out his arms and she leaned down to be enfolded in their warmth. A space inside her that she didn't even know had been empty filled with his love. Tears welled in her eyes, but she blinked them away. She refused to cry in front of Stetson again.

"I've missed you, Daddy," she said. "I'm sorry I didn't get home sooner."

He patted her back. "There's no need to be sorry. I'm just fine."

She drew back. "No you're not. Or you wouldn't be in a wheelchair."

"I shouldn't be. The dang doctor is just an overly cautious young whelp. All I need is a set of crutches and I'll get around just fine."

Lily went to argue, but Stetson beat her to it. "You'll have plenty of time to be on crutches, Theo. Right now you need to take it easy and let that leg heal. I'm sure Lily will be happy to wait on you hand and foot." The sarcasm in his voice was easy to read. At least it was for her. Her father didn't seem to notice.

"Lily has better things to do than take care of me. She's a big writer, you know."

"So I hear," Stetson said dryly. "But I think she can take a few days off from doodling cartoon characters to care for her daddy."

Doodling cartoon characters? Lily gritted her teeth.

"Thanks for bringing Daddy to the cottage, Stetson. But I can take it from here."

He cocked his head. "Can you?"

She had never been a physical person, but at that moment, she had a strong urge to pop Stetson right in the nose. Instead, she scowled up at him. In her heels, she had been able to look him in the eye without craning her neck too much. In bare feet, she felt like a little kid looking up at a skyscraper. The oversized pajamas printed with pink poodles getting pedicures she wore didn't help. But she refused to back down.

"If you'll excuse us, my father and I have some catching up to do. And I'm sure you have some wild horses that need taming."

"Still afraid of horses, Lillian?"

She stared at him in surprise. How did he know? She'd thought no one but her mother had known about her fear. She forced a laugh. "Scared of horses? Now that would be strange since I grew up on a horse and cattle ranch."

Stetson studied her for a long moment before he released the handles of the wheelchair and stepped back. "Very strange." He patted her father on the shoulder. "Let me know if you need anything, Theo." He turned on a boot heel and left, the front door slamming closed behind him.

Lily released her breath. "I see Stetson is still an annoying control freak."

Her father chuckled. "I wouldn't say he's a control freak. It's a huge amount of responsibility running a ranch this big. Stetson just takes the job of caring for everyone on this ranch, including your old dad, seriously."

Since Stetson had done a much better job of taking care of her father than she had, Lily couldn't very well argue. "Are you hungry, Daddy? I could make you breakfast."

"I already ate at the big house, but I'll be happy to visit with you while you make yourself some."

She might've rolled him into the kitchen if she hadn't noticed the tightening of his features or the way he rubbed his thigh muscle as if in pain. She moved around the wheelchair and took the handles. "I'm not very hungry either. Why don't we get you in bed and get that leg propped up on some pillows."

Once in his room, she helped him out of the chair and into bed. As she carefully tucked pillows under his leg, she noticed the photographs that covered the top of his dresser. Photographs of her and her mother. Her heart tightened. "I'm sorry, Daddy, that I wasn't here for you after Mum died."

Her father's eyes widened. "What are you talking about? You were here for months after your mother passed. And I wouldn't have let you give up your scholarship to Oxford even if you had wanted to. You worked hard for that."

"But I could've come back here for the summers." She glanced around. "I shouldn't have let you deal with all the memories alone."

He took her hand and squeezed it. "There are a lot of memories here. But those memories don't make me sad, Lilliput. They make me realize what a special gift I was given. I don't ever want to forget the time I spent here with you and your mother." He hesitated. "And I understand why you didn't want to come back. You and your mother were two peas in a pod. You were always her little shadow. When she was gone, I knew how alone you felt. I'm sorry I didn't know how to fill that gap. Talking about feelings has never been my strong suit."

Lily sat down on the edge of the bed. "Mine either. And maybe that's something we should work on. We should start by being completely honest with each other. How do you really feel?" Her father started to speak, but she held up her hand. "The truth, Daddy."

Her father sighed and sank back into the pillows she'd just positioned behind his head. "Like I've been trampled by a herd of Black Angus. I could sure use one of those painkillers the doctor prescribed. Stetson didn't get them when he took me up to the big house. And I didn't want to make a fuss."

"It's not a fuss, Daddy. People who care about you want to help you when you need it."

She couldn't deny Stetson cared about her father. He might not like her—and she certainly didn't like him—but he loved her dad. For that reason, she would try to get along with him while she was here.

She examined the prescription bottles on the nightstand. Once she found the painkillers, she tapped out a tablet and handed it and the half-empty bottle of water to her father. She waited for him to take the medication before pulling the sheet over his propped-up leg and gently tucking it around his waist.

"Now you just rest while I make you a cup of

tea." Her father might be more Texas now than English, but he still loved a good cup of tea. She gave him a kiss on the forehead, then turned for the door.

"Lilliput?"

She turned to find his eyes wet with tears.

"I'm glad you came home."

Her heart squeezed with guilt and love as her eyes welled. "I'm glad I did too, Daddy."

Tears filled her eyes even more when she stepped into the kitchen and a wash of memories assailed her. Her mother standing at the farmhouse sink doing dishes. Her mother at the butcher block island chopping vegetables. Her mother pulling cookies, which she called biscuits, out of the oven. And when Lily looked out the window to the garden, even more memories flooded in.

The garden had been her mother's. The Kingmans owned it. Her father had worked in it. But it had been Gwen who designed and made it what it was: a beautiful English garden set smack dab in the middle of a Texas ranch. All different kind of flowers, scrubs, and trees bloomed in a profusion of spring colors. Stone pathways wound their way through the beauty, each leading to a different area: the quaint dining table and chairs, the fire pit and a grouping of stone benches, the hammock hanging between two flowering cherry trees, and the stairs leading to the hedge labyrinth. Amid the flowers were bronze sculptures of every champion quarter horse the ranch had ever produced.

As Lily stood there taking in all the memories, she realized this was why she hadn't wanted to come home. It hurt too much. And yet, beneath the pain, there was also remembered joy. Her mother swinging her in the hammock, playing hide-and-seek with her in the labyrinth, teaching her how to plant tulip bulbs or prune a rose bush. But mostly Lily remembered the stories her mother told her. Stories of fairies and woodland creatures that lived in an English forest far, far away.

The fairies were mischievous, clever, and daring. Everything Lily wanted to be but wasn't. Which is why she had loved the stories and soaked them up like a dried-out sponge, begging her mother to tell them over and over again until Lily knew them by heart.

Everyone thought Lily was the creative genius behind Fairy Prairie. But in actuality, all she'd done was draw the pictures. The stories were the ones Gwen Daltry had made up for her shy, introverted daughter. Lily had just changed the English forest to a Texas prairie. Instead of sleeping in oak tree hollows, the fairies slept in sagebrush and mesquite. She had never intended to take credit for the stories. But when the book sold, her publishers had thought it would be less confusing for children if she just used her name on the cover.

But soon, she'd have to tell the world about her farce. Lily had run out of her mother's stories. Try as she might, she couldn't come up with another one. But she couldn't worry about that now. Now she needed to concentrate on taking care of her father.

While the kettle heated, she moved to the china cabinet to select a teapot and cups. The family heirlooms had been passed down from great-grandmothers and great-aunts. As Lily set one flowered china cup on its matching saucer, she remembered a conversation she'd once had with her mother.

"I don't want a special cup, Mum. What if I break it?"

Her mother had smiled softly. "A teacup you never drink from has no purpose, Lily Leigh. If you should break it while enjoying a tea party with your mother, then its life ended doing what it was meant to do. And what can be more special than that?"

The words had held no meaning to a five-year-old except she knew her mother wouldn't get mad if she broke the cup. Now Lily realized Mum's lesson had been much deeper. Gwen had ended her life doing what she loved to do—making a garden people would enjoy long after she was gone. What could be more special than that?

"Lily Leigh!"

Lily jumped, rattling the teacup against the saucer as she spun around. She only caught a quick glimpse of Delaney Kingman's grinning face before she was pulled into her arms for a tight hug. Delaney had always been a big, strong cowgirl, and it looked like she'd become even stronger in the last eight years. She seemed to be completely unaware of the fact that she was squeezing all the air out of Lily.

"Good to have you home, girl." Delaney's arms tightened even more as she lifted Lily clear off her feet. "I thought you'd left the ranch for good."

Spots started to form in front of Lily's eyes. She tried to speak, but the spots converged to black. She woke to find herself lying on the floor of the kitchen with the teakettle whistling and, not one, but two Kingmans leaning over her.

"You okay there, Lily?" Delaney gave her a none-too-gentle smack on the cheek.

"Jesus, Del!" Buck shoved his sister's hand away. "First, you almost squeeze the life out of her and now you're thumping her like a ripe watermelon. Can't you see she's fragile?" His gaze returned to Lily and his eyes looked a little dazed. "She's like a beautiful delicate flower that needs to be handled with care."

Delaney rolled her eyes. "Why do men go ga-ga over petite, delicate women? Who wants to roll around in bed with a fragile flower that can't even take a good hug?"

"Shut up, Del! How many times do I have to tell you that I don't want to talk about sex with my sister." He leaned closer to Lily. "She still looks like she's struggling to breathe. Maybe I should give her mouth-to-mouth." Before Buck could lean closer, the whistling of the teakettle stopped and Stetson's voice boomed.

"What the hell is going on here?"

Buck got to his feet. "Del almost killed Lily."

Delaney stood. "I wasn't trying to kill Lily. I was just happy to see her. I didn't think a little ol' hug would cause her to faint."

"She fainted?" Stetson appeared. Before she could sit up, he scooped her into his arms and plopped her in a kitchen chair. "Get her some water, Del."

"I don't need water," Lily said.

Stetson reached out and tipped up her chin. The warmth of his fingers had heat flooding her face. "Never mind, Del," he said. "Her color's coming back."

Delaney moved next to her big brother. "You okay, girl? You had me worried for a second."

"I'm fine, Del."

"You can say that again." Buck flashed Lily a smile. He had been a skinny teenager when Lily had left. Now he was as handsome as his brothers. But while Wolfe and Stetson had dark hair, Buck's was as blond as Adeline's. If any Kingman looked like a golden prince, it was Buck.

"Hello, Buck," she said. "It's nice to see you again."

His grin got even bigger. "The feeling is mutual. Are you sure you're okay? Maybe you should lie down . . . I have a great big ol' bed that I'd be happy to—"

Stetson shot him a warning look. "Buck."

"What? I was just being hospitable."

"Go be hospitable to the buyers who are showing up today to buy Majestic Glory's new foal."

"But—"

"Get going."

Buck's eyes narrowed. For a second, Lily thought he might argue. But then he grabbed the cowboy hat off the island and tugged it on. When he turned to her, he was all sparkling blue eyes and a flirty smile. "I better get to work, Lily. But I'll stop by later to see if you'd like to go for a little twilight horseback ride."

The thought of getting on a horse had Lily feeling like she might faint again. Before she had to come up with an excuse, Stetson stepped in.

"Lily is here to help her father, not go for twilight rides. Now get moving."

Buck sent him a glare before he headed out the side kitchen door.

"I better get too," Delaney said. "We're breeding today." She winked at Lily. "And you can't keep a good stud waiting. But I do want to catch up. How long are you staying for, Lily?"

Again, Stetson spoke for her. "Just a few days."

Lily *had* planned to stay only a few days. But that was before she realized how injured her father was. Before she realized memories weren't painful as much as bittersweet. Before she realized how much she'd missed home.

"Actually," she said. "I think I'll stay awhile."

# CHAPTER FOUR

STETSON SPENT THE MORNING IN the stables making sure everything went well breeding the new mare with one of their prized thoroughbred studs. Then he walked over to the old barn to see how the roof was coming along.

The entire roof had gone up in flames in the recent arson fire, along with the north corner of the barn where it looked like the fire had been started. Except for the doves that roosted in the rafters, no animals had been in the old barn at the time. All the horses were in the newer horse stables or grazing in the pastures, along with Delaney's herd of goats. The herding dogs, Raleigh and Dex, slept in the bunkhouse. If they had been sleeping in the barn, the arsonist wouldn't have made it past the door.

Of course, the dogs might have ended up dead.

The mutilation of an old longhorn bull proved that whoever was stirring up trouble on the ranch didn't mind killing animals. Bobby Tom had been on the ranch for close to twenty years. When Stetson saw that Bobby Tom had been shot in the head and the word JUSTICE carved into the bull's underbelly, he'd wanted his own justice.

He still did.

What kind of demented fool would think justice was served by carving up an animal and burning down a barn? And why did the sick bastard mean by *justice*? Who was the message for? The entire Kingman family? Or just one? If that were the case, which one?

Adeline was too sweet to have any enemies. Buck's easygoing charm had him making friends wherever he went. Delaney's bluntness could tick people off, but only until they found out she had a heart the size of Texas. Which left Stetson and Wolfe. Wolfe was charming with the ladies, but he had a bad temper that had landed him in the county jail on more than one occasion. He could easily have pissed someone off in a bar fight . . . or seduced someone's lady.

And Wolfe wasn't the only Kingman who pissed people off.

Running a ranch wasn't easy and sometimes there were tough choices. Stetson had fired his fair share of trainers and saddle tramps for not doing their jobs, for causing trouble in the bunkhouse, or for getting out of line with his sisters. But he'd gone through the list of people he'd fired over the years, and while a few had gotten angry about being let go, none had gone psycho.

Maybe they'd just hidden their anger well.

Something Stetson wasn't good at.

"Who you pissed off at today, Boss?"

The words pulled him out of his dark thoughts, and he glanced up to see his foreman climbing down from the scaffolding. For a big, muscle-bound guy, Gage Reardon was extremely agile. When he reached the lower level of the scaffolding, he grabbed a crossbar and gracefully swung down to the ground.

He pushed back his beat-up black cowboy hat and squinted in the morning sun. "You find out who did it?"

Stetson shook his head. "But when I do . . ."

Gage nodded. "You better not leave me out, Boss. You get first crack, but I want second."

"If there's anything left," Stetson said dryly before he glanced up at the men working on the roof. "How's it going?"

"Surprisingly, the storm last night didn't do that much damage. We should have it finished in the next week."

The "we" included Gage. His idea of over-seeing a job was working right along with his crew. This philosophy had garnered him a lot of respect. Not only from the men and women who worked for him, but also from Stetson. After only eight months of working on the ranch, Gage had become his right-hand man. Stetson loved his brothers, but he couldn't always count on them. He knew he could count on Gage to do anything.

Even things Stetson had no business asking a foreman to do.

"I need you to keep Buck busy for the next week or so. I'm talking so busy that he only has enough energy to fall into bed at night. I'd do it myself, but he doesn't listen to me as well as he does you."

Gage studied him for a second before he nodded. "Yes sir, Boss."

Stetson could've left it at that. Gage never expected an explanation. Still, Stetson felt like he deserved one. "Theo Daltry's daughter is back home to take care of him, and I don't want Buck sniffing after her like a dog in heat."

"I saw her pull in last night."

Stetson was surprised. "You were up?"

"Right up there." Gage pointed to the top of the scaffolding. "I figured it was the best place to keep an eye on things."

"You were up there all night? In the storm?"

Gage shrugged. "I've never minded a little rain. And I don't sleep real well anyway. When I saw the rental car pull in, I thought we might have our guy. By the time I got down from the scaffolding and to the cottage, there was no one around. So I did a little snooping and discovered a purse in the car with a passport inside. A few minutes later, you both came down the path. I figured you had things under control, so I went back to my lookout." He hesitated. "I take it this Lillian Daltry is trouble."

With a capital T. It was Stetson's fault that trouble was staying longer than just a few days. He should've kept his big mouth shut. Instead, he'd guilted Lily into staying longer. Now Buck was panting after her. If she were any other woman, Stetson might've taken Buck's interest with a grain of salt. Every other week, Buck was in love with a new woman. But Daltry women were different. They had a way of making men lose all touch with reality. Stetson wouldn't allow that to happen to his little brother.

"Thanks for keeping Buck busy, Gage," he said. "And for keeping an eye on things. I appreciate it."

"That's what you pay me for, Boss." Gage pulled the leather gloves from his back pocket and tugged them on. "Now I better get back to that roof."

"You got an extra hammer?" Stetson asked.

Gage grinned. "I think we can find one lying around."

Stetson spent the next few hours working on the roof in the late March sun before he headed to the house to catch up on some paperwork. On the way, he stopped in the garden to hose off some of his sweat.

He'd never liked the garden. Not only because of Gwen Daltry, but also because English gardens belonged in Texas as much as a castle did. It was just another example of his grandfather wanting to be something he wasn't. He wasn't a king. He'd just been a cowboy who knew how to make money. Having money wasn't all it was cracked up to be.

Stetson stripped off his shirt before he turned on the hose. Once he'd rinsed off, he turned off the spigot and shook like a dog. A startled gasp had him turning to see Lily sitting in the hammock.

Last night, she'd looked like a city girl in her classy white dress and skyscraper heels. This morning, she'd looked like a little girl in her baggy poodle pajamas and mussed hair. This afternoon, she looked like a sexy Daisy Duke in her tight t-shirt and cut-off shorts. Her legs were stretched out on the hammock, her bare feet with their soft-pink painted toes resting on the ropes. On her lap was a sketch pad filled with drawings of fairies . . . their images distorted by water droplets.

"Sorry," he said. "I didn't see you there."

"Obviously." She sent him an annoyed look.

He pointed to the picture. "Is it ruined?"

"It doesn't matter. They're just cartoon characters."

Her sarcasm and choice of words weren't lost on him. He figured she hadn't liked him referring to her fairies as cartoons. As he looked at the drawing, he had to admit the fairies didn't look cartoonish. They looked like art. Even spattered with water droplets, he could tell each fairy had its own personality and features. Some were thin and some were plump. Some had short hair and some had long. Some had bright smiles and others looked serious.

But there was one fairy in particular Stetson was looking for. Before he could find him, Lily flipped the sketch pad closed. It was obvious he had intruded on her creative space and she would just as soon he leave. But his curiosity got the best of him.

"Why fairies?" he asked.

Her eyebrows lifted. "Do you have something against fairies too?"

He didn't address the "too." She was right. He

did have something against her. As wrong as it may be to blame her for her mother's sins, he did.

"I just don't know why you wouldn't choose something different to write about," he said. "Whoever heard of a ranch of fairies that ride dragonflies and rope beetles?"

She looked surprised, and he realized his mistake. "How do you know they ride dragonflies and rope beetles?"

He shrugged and lied. "Your father talks a lot about your books."

She lifted her chin. "There's nothing wrong with my stories. I've won awards for giving children a creative, magical world to enjoy. But you wouldn't understand that because you were never a child. You were born old."

She was wrong. He hadn't been born old, but he'd had a very short childhood. It had ended when he'd turned ten and his mother had passed away. When she died, she took Stetson's belief in magic with her.

"You're right," he said. "I don't believe in fairytales. Or in making kids believe that life always has a happy ending."

She studied him for a moment before she spoke. "So you're not happy, Stetson? I would think owning all this—" she waved a hand around— "would make anyone happy."

So money was important to Lily. Just like it had been important to her mother. Gwen Daltry had set her sights on a rich Kingman. Stetson was going to make sure Lily didn't do the same.

"You can leave anytime you're ready, Lily. I can

keep an eye on Theo."

Her eyes registered surprise before they filled with suspicion. Their color perfectly matched the green of the garden. With her thick black tousled hair and petite features, she could be one of her beautiful fairies.

"Thanks, but as you so thoroughly pointed out, it's my job. Were you the one who found him after he fell off the ladder?"

"No. He wasn't here when he fell."

Her eyes widened. "Where was he?"

Stetson wasn't sure how much Theo wanted his daughter to know so he kept his answer vague. "In town."

"What was he doing on a ladder in town?"

Stetson shrugged. "You'll have to ask him."

She crossed her arms. "I will." But Stetson had to wonder if she would. She and Theo didn't seem to communicate very well. Which surprised him. He had no trouble talking to Theo. Theo was a good listener who always had sound advice. But maybe talking was easier when you weren't a father and his child. Parent-child relationships were more complicated. His relationship with Douglas had certainly been. He blamed Gwen Daltry for that.

He picked up his hat and shirt from the nearby bench. "Well, I'll let you get back to your cartoons." He could almost feel her glare burning into his back as he walked away.

He was halfway up the path that led to the big house when a mud-spattered dually truck came barreling up the driveway. Stetson cussed under his breath as the truck came to a gravel-spitting stop. The window rolled down and Wolfe stuck his head out.

"Is there a reason you're wandering around half-naked, big bro?"

"Is there a reason you're back from the stock show so early? I thought you were staying in Dallas through the weekend."

Wolfe pulled off his aviator sunglasses and tucked them into the neckband of his t-shirt. He was the only one in the family with their mother's gray eyes. The combination of his light gray eyes and long, dark hair gave him a wolfish look.

"There wasn't any good horseflesh worth sticking around for," he said.

"That never stopped you from staying to do some big-city carousing."

Wolfe flashed a toothy grin. "True, but this time I had trouble keeping my mind on women. Anything else happen while I was gone?"

"No, but I have a feeling it will."

Wolfe's smile faded. "Yeah, me too. Which is why I came back—" He cut off as his gaze zeroed in on something over Stetson's shoulder. By the hungry gleam that entered his brother's eyes, Stetson figured Lily had come out from the garden to investigate. A quick glance over his shoulder confirmed it.

"Who is that?" Wolfe asked.

Stetson sighed. "Lily Daltry."

"No shit?" Wolfe quickly turned off his truck and hopped out.

Stetson stepped in front of him. "You can talk

to Lily later. Now, I'd like you to give me the details of the stock show."

Unlike Buck, Wolfe completely ignored Stetson and stepped around him. He pulled off his cowboy hat and smiled the slow, lazy smile he reserved for all his conquests. "Why if it isn't Lily Daltry. What brings you to the great state of Texas, darlin'?"

The afternoon breeze lifted Lily's hair and fluttered it around her face. She didn't push it back. She seemed to be frozen in place. Wolfe's dark good looks did that to women. Left them stunned. When he was younger, Stetson had been jealous of his brother's ability. Now, he was too busy to worry about stunning woman. He had a woman in Amarillo he got together with occasionally who liked his looks well enough. That worked for him. What didn't work for him was Wolfe setting his sights on Lily.

Especially when Lily had always had her sights set on Wolfe. Her childhood crush had been more than obvious. Finding her naked in bed waiting for Wolfe hadn't been all that surprising. It had confirmed his belief that Daltrys were willing to do anything to get a Kingman.

"Lily's here helping Theo until he gets on his feet," Stetson said. "We should let her get back to—"

"Would you stop that!" Lily cut him off. "I can talk for myself."

He turned to her. "Not from what I've seen."

She crossed her arms and glared at him. "Because you never give people a chance to talk.

You just butt in like the bully you are."

Wolfe laughed. "Looks like she's got you figured out, Stet." He flashed his lazy smile at Lily. "But I hope you don't lump me with my big brother. I've never bullied a woman in my life."

"No, you only seduce them," Lily said. "Which is a form of bullying. Bullies use their brute strength to get people to do what they want. Seducers use their good looks and charm."

Wolfe's eyes widened in surprise and it was Stetson's turn to laugh. "Looks like I'm not the only one she's figured out."

Wolfe recovered from his shock and grinned. "That's okay. I like my women feisty."

"I'm not your woman," Lily said. "Now if you'll excuse me, I have to check on my father."

When she was gone, Wolfe released a low whistle. "Damn, Lily's grown into one fine-looking woman. I'm glad I came back early."

Stetson's muscles tighten as he turned to his brother. "Stay away from her, Wolfe."

"You challenging me, bro?"

"Stay away from her."

Wolfe stared at him in confusion. "You've never warned me away from any woman before. Why are you suddenly—" He cut off, and a sparkle entered his eyes. "Wait a second, don't tell me that Lily has finally caught the attention of the Monk of Kingman Ranch."

"Not likely."

"Are you sure? There certainly seem to be some sexual sparks flying between you two."

There were sparks. Just not of the sexual variety.

Stetson was about to say that when a thought struck him. He'd been wondering how he was going to keep Wolfe and Buck away from Lily. Wolfe had just handed him the perfect solution. His brothers had only two rules where women were concerned:

No married women.

And never go after a woman your brother was interested in.

Lying didn't set well with Stetson. But if it protected his family, he was willing to tell a little white lie. Or just play along.

"It's hard not to be interested. Lily has become a beautiful woman." That wasn't a lie.

Wolfe nodded. "She sure as hell has. A man would be a fool not to go after her." He thumped Stetson on the shoulder. "So stop being a damned fool and go after her if you want her. I'll back off."

"Buck likes her too."

"I'll handle Buck. He's had his fair share of girls. You're the one who needs a woman in a bad way." Wolfe grinned. "Maybe good sex will improve your disposition."

"What's wrong with my disposition?"

"Nothing . . . if you like rattlesnakes." Wolfe slung an arm around his brother's shoulders. "Good thing women don't mind a little rattling and a nip or two. Now let's get some sweet tea and I'll tell you how to go about catching a Lily. And stripping off your shirt was a good start. She seemed to have trouble taking her eyes off you."

# CHAPTER FIVE

AFTER CHECKING ON HER FATHER, Lily went back to the garden and tried to finish her sketch. But she'd lost her focus. Every time she looked up and saw the hose lying on the ground, a vision of Stetson without his shirt popped into her head. Finally, she gave up on seeing if drawing her fairies would inspire a new story and flipped the page to a blank sheet of paper. The best way to get an image out of her head was to sketch it.

Her hand moved with lightning speed as she drew every feature and muscle. Stetson had plenty of muscles. He had muscles in places Lily didn't even know you could have muscles. They stacked like building blocks up his torso, starting at the waistband of his worn jeans and ending at his strong corded neck.

He had a rancher's tan. The skin of his face, neck, and lower arms were a toasty caramel while the skin of his torso and upper arms were a lighter vanilla cream. His hair had always been a dark brown. But today, she had noticed the sun-lightened whiskey-colored strands interwoven with the deep chocolate.

His face was a collage of hard angles and harsh lines. Deep set eyes and a roman nose. Stern lips and a square chin. High cheekbones and faint scars.

Once she was finished, Lily examined her work. She had planned to do a quick sketch, but the drawing was much more detailed than she'd intended.

And much more sensual.

Shirtless Stetson could easily grace the cover of a steamy romance novel. While he wasn't as handsome as his brothers, he had a rugged, edgy quality that made a woman think of tousled bed sheets and hot sex. Just looking at the drawing had Lily's body feeling flush.

"It's sure a hot one."

Lily startled and flipped her sketch pad closed.

Wolfe stood at the edge of the rose garden with his cowboy hat in hand. If possible, he was even more handsome than she remembered. His black hair seemed even blacker and his gray eyes more intense. As a teenager, she had dedicated pages and pages of her diary to the unique color of those eyes. When he'd turned them on her, she'd been unable to breathe or think. Wolfe had been the perfect prince in all her teenage fantasies. Even more so after her mother had passed. Focusing on Wolfe had helped keep Lily's grief at bay.

Which is how she had ended up naked in his bed on graduation night.

Or a bed she had thought was his.

But his pretty gray eyes and handsome features no longer made her heart beat faster or her knees turn to water. As an adult, she realized how silly she'd been to be so enamored of him. And how young and stupid she'd been to want to give her virginity to a boy who had never even asked her on a date. She was lucky she had chosen the wrong bedroom. Although at the time she'd only felt humiliated and embarrassed at being caught naked in Stetson's bed.

She still felt a little embarrassed. Had Stetson told Wolfe? Probably. They were brothers after all. They'd probably had a good laugh about Lily's failed attempt at seduction. But she wasn't that same awestruck girl anymore.

"Hello, Wolfe," she said. "Still breaking girls' hearts?"

"Never my intention."

"Then you are."

"I try not to." He moved closer. "I hope I didn't break yours."

So Stetson had told him. Or maybe it had just been blatantly obvious. She *had* been broken hearted that Wolfe hadn't returned her affections, but her hurt had quickly dwindled after leaving the ranch. "Childhood crushes are easily gotten over," she said.

He placed his hat over his heart. "Ouch. You wound me."

She laughed. "I doubt it. I'm sure you have plenty of women still crushing on you."

He winked. "But none as beautiful as you."

"You're a hopeless flirt, Wolfe Kingman. If you thought I was so beautiful, why didn't you ask me out?"

He took a seat on the stone bench across from the hammock. "Because my family has strict rules about being respectful to the people who work for us and not mixing business with pleasure."

"I didn't work for you."

"Your daddy does."

"And if he didn't, you would've been interested?"

He hesitated and then answered honestly. "No. You were a little too innocent. I do have a few morals where women are concerned." He crossed a boot over his knee and hooked his hat on the toe. "So tell me what you've been doing while you've been gone. I hear you've become a big-time writer."

"I don't know if I'd call myself a big-time writer, but my children's books have been doing well. Well enough to pay the bills."

His eyebrows lifted. "Then you are doing well. I heard life in England isn't cheap. Why England? I know you went to college there, but why did you stay?"

Since he had been truthful, she was too. "Because it was far away from Texas and the memories of my mom I wanted to forget."

He studied her for a moment before he nodded. "Yeah. Memories of moms can hurt like hell."

That's what she'd thought. But since coming back home, she'd found comfort in making tea in the same kitchen her mother had. And in sketching where she and her mom had talked and laughed and made a fairy garden.

"Not all memories hurt," she said. "But it's hard

losing your mother. And you and your brothers and sisters were so young when you lost yours."

Elizabeth Kingman had died when Lily was five. She had no memories of the woman, but she'd seen pictures of her in the big house. Adeline and Buck looked like their mother. She'd been beautiful and almost ethereal with light blond hair and clear sky-blue eyes.

"Being young might've made it easier," Wolfe said. "I don't remember much about her. Stet, on the other hand, remembers everything. Since my dad didn't like to talk about her after she passed, I think Stetson felt like he had to keep her memory alive. He used to tell us stories about her every night before we went to bed."

Lily had a hard time envisioning Stetson telling bedtime stories to his brothers and sisters, and her feelings must've shown on her face because Wolfe laughed.

"Yeah, I know. It's hard to see Stetson as a sentimental guy. But underneath all his grumpiness, he's sensitive." Wolfe studied her. "So are you dating anyone in England?"

The abrupt subject change had her blinking. "Uhh . . . no."

"Just getting out of a serious relationship?"

Lily had never been in a serious relationship. In college, she had gone out a few times with a young man in one of her literature classes. After moving to Surrey, she'd dated a waiter who worked at the café she frequented. But neither relationship had moved to the serious stage. She wondered why Wolfe was asking. There seemed to be only one answer.

"No," she said. "I'm not just getting out of a serious relationship. And I'm not interested in getting into one either. Nor am I interested in having a fling with you, Wolfe."

He laughed. "That's good. I think we'll make better friends than lovers."

"Is that your way of getting past my defenses? Act like friends and then seduce me into your bed?"

"No, but that's a great idea. I might have to try that one." He winked. "Just not on you." He stood. "Listen, Potts is making his famous chicken enchiladas tonight. Why don't you come up to the house for dinner?"

Lily's mouth salivated at just the thought of the Kingman's cook's enchiladas. It had been a long time since she'd had good Tex-Mex. Unfortunately, she had other obligations. "I can't. I need to stay with my daddy."

"Theo's welcome too."

"Thank you, but I think he should rest." She paused. "But you could bring me leftovers."

"You got it." He pulled on his hat and tapped the brim. "See ya later, Lily Leigh."

"Not if I see you first, Wolfgang Rudolph."

He cringed. "Okay, let's make a pact right now to never use our middle names."

She laughed. "What? You don't like Rudolph? But it's so cute. Goodbye, Rudy. Let me know if any mean kids won't let you play their reindeer games."

"Smartass." He turned and headed down the

path. "Now I'm going to keep all the leftover enchiladas to myself."

"I take it back," she called after him.

"Too late. All those tortilla rolls of cheesy chicken goodness are mine." He laughed evilly. "All mine."

"You're a mean man, Rudolph!"

The only reply was more evil laughter as he disappeared around the side of the cottage.

Once Wolfe was gone, Lily headed into the house to check on her father.

He was awake and seemed to feel much better. She attributed that to the pain pill so she gave him another one with the BLT she made him for lunch. He spent the rest of the afternoon napping while she sat in the chair next to him and tried to come up with a new storyline for her next Fairy Prairie book.

Nothing came to her. Not one thing.

What would she do if she couldn't come up with a new story? Writing and illustrating children's books was all she knew how to do. All she wanted to do. She could be just an illustrator and let other people write the story. But the thought of doing illustrations for someone else's stories seemed all wrong.

A knock on the front door pulled her out of her depressed musings. She got up and went to answer it. She thought it might be Delaney coming to catch up. Or Wolfe with a plate of enchiladas. Or even Stetson stopping by to check on her father.

Instead, it was Vivian Fletcher.

"Mrs. Fletcher?" Lily couldn't hide her surprise at seeing her third-grade teacher on the front stoop.

"Lillian!" Mrs. Fletcher shifted the tote bags she carried and pulled Lily into her plump body for a one-armed hug. "It's so good to see you. Your daddy was thrilled when he found out you were coming." She released Lily and held up the tote bags. "I figured you probably hadn't had a chance to go to the grocery store, so I picked up a few things for you and Theo at the Cursed Grocery Mart."

"Thank you so much." Lily stepped back. "Won't you come in?" She couldn't remember Mrs. Fletcher ever coming to the cottage, but she must have visited after Lily left for college because she carried the bags straight to the kitchen.

"I didn't know what you liked so I just stuck to the basics and your father's favorites." Mrs. Fletcher set the bags on the counter and started putting the grocery items away while Lily watched with confusion. How did Mrs. Fletcher know her father's favorites? And her way around the kitchen?

"How was your trip?" Mrs. Fletcher continued as she put a box of Earl Grey tea in the cupboard. "Did you run into any turbulence? The one and only time I've been on a plane was when I went to a science workshop for elementary school teachers in Seattle. On the way home, the plane ran into a storm. By the time we landed and I got off, I swore I would never fly again. I didn't. But being a big famous writer, you probably travel all the time and are used to a little turbulence."

Mrs. Fletcher beamed at Lily as she put a carton of Lily's father's favorite mint chocolate chip ice cream in the freezer. "I'm so proud of you, honey. You always were one of my brightest and most creative students. I would love for you to come talk to my class about your creative writing process."

Lily had no writing process. Just a good memory. And that memory had run out of stories. But she couldn't say no to one of her favorite teachers. Especially when it looked like she'd been so kind to Theo.

"Of course. I'd love to come talk to your students." She started helping Mrs. Fletcher put away the groceries. When they were finished, Mrs. Fletcher folded her tote bags and tucked them under her arm.

"How's your father doing today? I've been worried sick about him since he fell fixing my porch light. I should've thrown that rickety ladder away years ago. But it was Garland's and after he passed, I struggled to throw anything of his away."

So that's how her father had fallen. He had been helping Mrs. Fletcher. Why hadn't he just said so? Her father had always helped out the people of Cursed whenever they needed a hand. It made sense he would help a widow who had lost her husband no more than a year ago.

"I was sorry to hear about Mr. Fletcher," Lily said.

Mrs. Fletcher smiled sadly. "Garland was a good

man. But the Lord certainly taught me a lesson when your daddy fell off that old ladder. Let go of the past or you'll never be able to embrace the future." Her eyes softened as she looked at Lily. "I know how close you were to your mother. I just want you to know I'll never replace her in your father's heart. Just like he won't replace Garland in mine. But we've discovered the heart has plenty of room for old and new love." She gave Lily another tight hug. "Now I better go check on your daddy."

After she left the room, Lily stood there feeling stunned. Her father and her third-grade teacher were in love? But her father hadn't said a word about Mrs. Fletcher. Not one word. He'd mentioned Garland Fletcher passing away, but that was it. Lily felt blindsided and more than a little hurt.

She waited for Mrs. Fletcher to leave before she headed to her father's room. The sheepish look on his face said it all.

"Why didn't you tell me you were seeing Vivian Fletcher, Daddy?" she asked.

"I planned to. But I guess I was worried you'd be upset."

She sat down on the edge of the bed. "I'm an adult, Dad. I can deal with you dating. Mom has been gone for almost nine years now."

He cleared his throat. "Vivian and I aren't just dating, Lilliput. I've asked her to marry me."

# CHAPTER SIX

UNLESS THEY HAD GUESTS, SUPPER-TIME at the Kingman house was served buffet style in the kitchen. Everyone filled a plate with whatever Ralph Potter, or Potts as they called him, was serving and then sat down at the big harvest table to eat.

Stetson much preferred eating in the kitchen to the grand dining room. After a long hard day of work, he enjoyed savoring a beer and whatever delicious food Potts had prepared, and listening to his siblings talk about their day and rib each other.

Although he didn't enjoy it so much when he was the focus of that ribbing.

"Stetson has a girlfriend," Buck said in an annoying singsong voice.

All eyes turned to him. Stetson glared at Wolfe, who only shrugged. "Hey, I was only clearing the path for you, bro. I also invited her to dinner tonight, but she declined."

The last thing Stetson needed was Wolfe try-ing to play matchmaker. Especially when he had no intention of being matched up with Lily. "I'll do my own inviting," he said. "I don't need your help."

"I'm going to have to disagree with that. You haven't dated in years. You need all the help you can get."

"Wait a minute." Delaney swallowed the bite of enchiladas she'd just taken. "Who are we talking about?"

"Lily Daltry," Adeline answered. Obviously, Wolfe hadn't just told Buck.

Delaney looked at Stetson. "Lily? Theo's daughter? But I thought you two didn't get along. When we were kids, you were always making her cry."

"Which is why he needs some expert help," Wolfe said. "He has a lot of atoning to do if he wants to get Lily into bed."

Adeline looked appalled. "You aren't just trying to get her into bed, are you, Stet? She's Theo's daughter."

Stetson sent Wolfe another warning look before he answered his sister. "As usual, Wolfe has sex on the brain. I'm not going to seduce Lily."

Buck perked up. "So you're not interested in her?" He turned to Wolfe. "What the hell, Wolfe? You weren't clearing the path for Stetson. You were clearing the path for yourself. And if you think I'm going to let a player like you have Lily, you can think again."

Wolfe looked thoroughly amused. "If I wanted Lily, you couldn't keep me away from her, little brother."

"The hell I couldn't!" Buck jumped up.

Stetson slammed a fist down on the table rattling

the glasses. "Enough! Sit down, Buck, and watch your mouth. Just because Mama and Daddy are gone doesn't mean you can use bad language at the dinner table." He pointed his fork at Wolfe. "And you quit stirring the pot. Like Addie said, she's Theo's daughter and should be respected." He paused to figure out how he could stake a claim on Lily without staking a claim. "But Wolfe is right. I do find Lily attractive." Not a lie. "And I would like to spend more time with her." A big lie.

"And try to get her into bed," Wolfe added.

Adeline huffed. "You do have sex on the brain, Wolfe. One day, you're going to meet a woman who isn't going to fall all over herself to please you. When you do, maybe you'll figure out women are more than just bodies made for your pleasure."

"Hey, I pleasure them too. I would never expect to get pleasure without giving it."

"How thoughtful," Adeline said sarcastically.

Buck cut in. "Well, if it doesn't work out between you and Lily, I get second dibs. I really think she could be my soul mate."

Delaney laughed. "You thought that about Kelly Smith and Georgia Clines and Delia Macintosh. Should I go on?"

"At least I like animals of the two-legged variety."

"I like people." Delaney paused. "I just like horses, dogs, and cats better."

"And goats," Buck said. "Let's not forget your stupid goats. That one you call Caesar ate my damn hat."

"You shouldn't have left it on the fencepost while you were digging that posthole. You know Caesar likes to try new things."

"Cowboy hats aren't goat food!"

Stetson changed the subject before the argument could get too heated. "How did the search for a new housekeeper go, Addie?"

Adeline blotted her mouth and set down her napkin. Unlike Wolfe, who always devoured his food, she had barely touched her enchiladas. "Not well. We didn't have one applicant. I think word has gotten out that we're not an easy family to work for."

"That's crazy," Delaney said. "We're the best family to work for. Isn't that right, Potts?"

Potts was standing at the sink washing dishes. As a former cowboy and trail cook, he never minced words. "Yep . . . if your idea of the best family is a pack of unruly wolves."

Wolfe laughed. "Could this wolf get some more enchiladas, Potts?"

After supper, the family usually dispersed. Addie would go up to her room. Wolfe and Buck would play pool in the basement or head to Nasty Jack's bar. And Delaney would go to the entertainment room and watch reruns of every horse movie ever made. Stetson usually caught up on paperwork in his office or read by the fire in the great room.

But tonight he felt a little too restless to do paperwork or read. So he decided to walk down to the stables and check on Majestic Glory's new foal.

The horse stables were quite a distance from the house and the shortest route was through the garden. Still, Stetson would've taken the long way around if the cottage hadn't been dark. Lily probably had jet lag and had gone to bed early.

He slipped into the garden and made his way along the path. The moon was only partially full, but it shone bright enough for Stetson to spot Lily's sketch pad sitting on the hammock. After a quick glance at the cottage to make sure the lights were still out, he picked up the sketch pad and flipped it open. But he didn't find sketches of fairies. Instead he found a sketch of a shirtless man.

He tilted the drawing toward the moonlight to get a better look and was surprised to recognize the man. It was him. At least the face was his. The body had twice as many muscles. He didn't know how long he stared at the picture before the hoot of an owl startled him. He dropped the sketch pad and jumped back, tripping over something behind him. He reached out to break his fall and ended up grabbing hold of a rosebush. The thorns sank into his hand like mini razor blades.

"Sonofabitch!" He released the bush and fell on his butt, knocking over the planter he'd fallen over.

The porch light came on.

He struggled to his feet and tried to make a run for it. But he forgot about the lights Theo had strung in the trees. They all lit up at once and he froze long enough for Lily to spot him.

"Stetson?"

He turned to find her standing in the open doorway of the cottage in her silly poodle pajamas. He lifted a hand that still stung from the thorns. "Sorry. I was just heading to the stables and I knocked over this planter."

"Oh no!" She hurried out the door and down the steps.

"I'm okay," he said. "No need to get upset."

But she didn't pay him one speck of attention. Instead, she knelt on the ground and searched through the potting soil that had spilled from the planter.

"What are you doing?" he asked as he pulled out a thorn and sucked on his finger.

"I'm looking for the fairy garden."

"The what?"

"Never mind. Just get out of here, you clumsy oaf, before you ruin something else."

He scowled down at her. "Hey, in case you've forgotten, this is my garden."

She frantically searched through the dirt. "But the fairy garden was my mother's."

Well, shit.

He knelt next to her and started searching through the dirt that covered the path. "Can you explain what I'm looking for?"

"Miniature things that would go in a garden. Hammock, bench, butterflies. Anything that will lure the fairies to come play." She lifted something from the dirt and brushed it off. It was a ceramic mushroom with a painted door and windows. The spotted cap had a long crack in it.

"I'll buy you a new one," Stetson said. "I'm sure they sell them on Amazon."

"No, they don't." She finished brushing the dirt off the mushroom. "My mother painted this one by hand."

He cringed. "Look, I'm sorry."

She lifted her gaze from the mushroom. "No, you're not. You've never been sorry for the mean things you've done to me."

"What mean things?"

"Putting garden snakes and toads in my playhouse. Telling the bus driver I was sick so she left without me and I was late for school. Knocking me into the pond in my new Easter dress."

"I did not knock you into the pond. You slipped."

"After you bumped into me."

"Purely an accident. And I helped you out."

"While you laughed hysterically. And maybe you didn't mean to push me into the pond, but I noticed you didn't deny the snakes and toads or making me miss the bus."

He couldn't. He'd put the reptiles and amphibians in her playhouse and lied to the bus driver about her being sick. He'd also pulled numerous other childish pranks on her. He just hadn't realized Lily knew he was responsible. No wonder she viewed him as a bully. He had been one. All because he had resented her mother. For a man who prided himself on being fair, he certainly hadn't been fair to Lily.

"I'm sorry," he said. "I was a punky kid who should've been taken out to the woodshed and had his butt warmed. My daddy would have if he'd ever found out." He studied her. "Why didn't you tell on me?"

She smoothed her hand through the potting soil and smiled sadly. "I guess I wanted to prove that I was as tough as the Kingmans—instead of the wimpy gardener's daughter who was afraid of her own shadow."

Stetson's guilt increased tenfold. But before he could apologize again, she noticed the drops of blood on his jeans. "What happened?"

"I shook hands with a rosebush."

She dusted the dirt from her hands. "Let me see?" She took his hand and leaned closer to examine his palm. Something warm unfurled in his stomach. Something he hadn't felt in a long time. The ponytail on the top of her head brushed his chin and the scent of floral shampoo and soft woman filled his nostrils. A tremble of need ran through him. A need so strong he couldn't resist lifting his other hand to slide it through the ebony waves. Thankfully, a sharp stab of pain pierced his palm and brought him back to his senses.

"Oww!" He jerked his hand from hers.

"Sorry," Lily said. "You still had a thorn. But it's out now."

He studied his stinging palm. "Thanks a lot. That hurt like hell."

She laughed. She had one of those musical laughs that sounded like chimes dancing in a spring breeze. "And here I thought Kingmans were so tough."

He lifted his gaze to find her eyes twinkling teasingly. The warm feeling returned. Again he had the urge to touch her. "And here I thought the gardener's daughter was so shy."

She pulled her gaze away from him and went back to sifting through the soil. "Then I guess we both aren't what we seem."

They continued to search until they'd found the rest of the fairy garden items: a yarn hammock, a miniature bench made of popsicle sticks, a handful of pebbles that had been used for the pathway, and three tiny metal butterflies no bigger than Lily's pinkie nail. The only thing that appeared to be damaged was the mushroom. Although once they repotted the flowering plant and restored the fairy garden beneath its big pink flowers and green leaves, the crack wasn't that noticeable.

"I never even knew we had a fairy garden," Stetson said.

Lily adjusted the miniature bench. "Because you were always too busy to spend much time here in the garden."

He hadn't been too busy. Just too resentful of the woman who lived in the cottage. He still was.

He stood and brushed the dirt from his jeans before holding out a hand to help Lily up. "Sorry again about the mushroom. Hopefully, the fairies won't put a curse on me for cracking their house."

She took his hand and allowed him pull her to her feet. "They might. Fairies are known to be short-tempered."

"Are yours?"

"Only one. Beetlebub is an angry fairy who is always making the other fairies' lives miserable." She studied Stetson. "But maybe he's just misunderstood."

*Let go of her hand and leave.* But for some reason—maybe a fairy curse—Stetson couldn't seem to let go of the soft hand he held. Or look away from the moonlight reflected in her vibrant green eyes. Those eyes drew him in, and before he knew it, he was tilting his head. But before he could do something extremely stupid, she stepped away.

"I better get back inside. Goodnight, Stetson."

He stood there and watched until she disappeared into the house. Then he picked up his cowboy hat from where it had fallen when he'd tripped and slapped it against his leg.

"Pull your head out, Stetson," he said. "She's not for you."

He tugged on his hat and headed to the stables.

When he got there, he found the doors open. Three months ago, that wouldn't have been strange. But since the fire and mutilation, Stetson had given strict orders about locking the doors at night. He slowed his stride and approached the open doors with caution. A dark form sat on the ground just inside.

"Who's there?" he asked.

"It's Tab, sir. Someone broke into the stables."

Stetson hurried over and knelt next to his stable manager. "You okay?"

"I'm fine." He rubbed the back of his head. "Just a bump on the head and a bruised ego for letting someone get the best of me."

"What happened?"

"Someone snuck up behind me and knocked me out cold. I didn't come to until Gage showed up."

Before Stetson could question him more, Gage appeared in the doorway. He looked thoroughly pissed. "I couldn't find any signs of the sonofa— hey, Boss. I just tried to call your cell phone."

Stetson reached in his back pocket for his phone, but it wasn't there. It must've fallen out in the garden. "What happened?" he asked.

"I don't know. I saw someone outside the stables from my perch on the scaffolding. By the time I got here, I found the doors open and Tab on the floor."

"The horses?"

"All okay. I think I scared whoever it was off before he could do anything." Gage paused. "But that doesn't mean he won't be back. And here's the interesting part, Boss. He didn't break in. There's no damage to the door. And it was locked earlier when I came by to check."

Stetson stared at Gage as the truth dawned. "So that's means that someone knew the security code."

Which meant they were dealing with an insider.

# CHAPTER SEVEN

"WHAT ARE YOU DOING OUT of bed, Daddy?" Lily hurried over to help her father, but he balanced on the crutches and held up a hand.

"I'm fine, Lilliput. It's been two days, and I'm about to go stir crazy lying around in that bed. I need to get up and move."

Lily sighed. "Fine, but I wish you'd stay in bed until I get back from town." She'd agreed to talk to Vivian Fletcher's class that afternoon . . . and while she was at it, find out exactly what was going on between her and Theo. As usual, her father hadn't given her much information about his relationship with Vivian. Which made Lily feel uneasy about him jumping into marriage.

"Stop worrying, honey," her father said. "I'm only going to sit out in the garden and get a little sun." He glanced at the clock on the wall. "Now hurry up or you'll be late. I'm sure those kids can't wait to meet a big-time writer."

Realizing that she was running late, she grabbed her purse and the tote bag she'd filled with books for the class. "Promise me you'll call one of the

Kingmans if you need anything."

"I promise. Now git."

She gave him a quick kiss on the cheek before she hurried out the door. She was on her way to her rental car when one of the Kingmans' many garage doors opened and a Ford pickup pulled out. She recognized it immediately. It was the same F150 truck Stetson had gotten as a high school graduation gift from his father. For a thirteen-year-old truck, it was in pristine condition. The red paint glistened in the sun like a polished apple.

The truck finished backing out and started down the road toward her. Stetson was driving and Wolfe sat in the passenger's seat. For a moment, she thought Stetson was going to drive right by without a greeting. But then the truck stopped next to her, and Wolfe rolled down his window.

Lily had never compared the two brothers before—probably because she'd always thought Wolfe was the most handsome. But when the two men turned to her, she realized her mistake. Wolfe's features might be perfect, but there was an intriguing beauty about imperfection too. A flower with one wilted petal. A deep blue sky with a smattering of dark clouds. A handsome man with a scarred cheek.

Today, Stetson wore a green and gold plaid western shirt and a brown felt hat. Beneath the brim, his dark eyes stared back at her. She had always thought of his eyes as coal black—or maybe cold black. But the sun spilling in through the windshield revealed them as a warm brown that made her think of the dark molasses cookies her mother used to make every Christmas.

"Hey, Lily." Wolfe's greeting pulled her attention from Stetson.

"Hi, Wolfe."

His gray eyes sparkled with humor. "I'm glad you remember my name." Before she could do more than blush at the realization that he'd caught her staring at his brother, he looked down at the tote bag she carried. "Where are you going? I hope you're not leaving us so soon."

"No. I'm headed into town. I'm talking at the elementary school today."

"Really? We're headed into town too. And we'd love you to join us." Before Lily could decline, he opened the door and got out. "There's just no sense wasting gas when we're both going to the same place."

"Thank you, Wolfe, but I'd rather drive myself."

"Nonsense. Who wants to drive alone when they can drive with friends?" He looked into the cab of the truck. "Ain't that right, Stet?"

It took a moment for Stetson to answer. "It would be our pleasure."

"See?" Wolfe held open the door and grinned at Lily. "You wouldn't want to take pleasure away from my brother, would you? Believe me when I tell you, he doesn't get a lot of it."

Unless she wanted to make a scene, Lily had no choice but to climb into the truck. Wolfe closed the door. But instead of getting into the back seat, he stepped away.

"Y'all have fun now."

"Wait," she said. "Aren't you coming with us?"

Wolfe shook his head. "I just remembered something I need to do. But Stet here will see you safely into town." Again, he glanced at his brother. "Won't you, Stet?"

This time, Stetson didn't say a word. He just hit the gas and left his brother in a cloud of dust.

"You don't have to take me," she said. "I'm perfectly capable of driving myself."

"It's fine."

She set her tote bag and purse on the floor and scrambled to get her seatbelt on as he took a corner fast. "You're not acting like it's fine."

He let up on the gas and released his breath. "I just don't like being manipulated by my brother."

She laughed, and Stetson shot her glance. "What's so funny?"

"I just think it's humorous that you don't like being controlled, but yet you like controlling everyone."

She expected him to argue, but instead he conceded. "I guess you have a point." He returned his attention to the road. "So whose class are you talking to?"

"Mrs. Fletcher's." She hesitated. "I guess you've heard about her and my father."

"I knew they were seeing each other," he said.

"You could've said something."

"It wasn't my place."

"Did he tell you he's asked her to marry him?"

"No. But I'm glad to hear it. They make a good couple. She's a good lady. Your father's a good man."

Her father *was* a good man and Mrs. Fletcher *was* a good woman. But that didn't mean they'd make a good couple. "Don't you think it's a little too soon for marriage? Mr. Fletcher has only been gone for a year."

He glanced over at her. "And your father has been alone for close to nine."

"He hasn't been alone. He's had me." Since she hadn't exactly been an attentive daughter, she quickly added, "And he has you and the entire Kingman family."

"You know it's not the same, Lily. Just because you have family around you, doesn't mean you don't get lonely."

She was stunned. Stetson was lonely? She'd never thought of him as the type of man who experienced those kinds of emotions. He seemed too detached. A loner who enjoyed his solitude. But wasn't that what people thought about her too? She was an introverted writer who enjoyed working away in her little cottage. And she did. But there were also times—a lot of times— when the loneliness was almost too much to bear. Maybe that's how her father felt too. Which could explain why he was rushing into marriage with Vivian.

"I still think it's too soon," she said.

"For them? Or for you?"

She started to say "them," but then realized that wasn't the truth. "Both. I've been a crappy daughter and I want time to make it up to my dad."

"And you think you won't have time if he marries Vivian?" Stetson looked at her. "There's a big difference between a daughter and a wife, Lily. Be his daughter. But let Vivian be his wife."

As they drove into town, she mulled over his words. She realized that most of her doubts about her father and Vivian had to do with one word. *Wife*. In her mind, her mother had always been her father's wife. It was hard to let that go.

Even when Lily knew she should.

The streets of Cursed had been named for all the catastrophes that had befallen the townsfolk throughout the last century and a half. Tornado ran through the center of town, and when Stetson headed under the highway bridge, there were the residential streets—Hailstorm, Locust, Drought, Starvation, Depression, Recession, Dust Bowl, Prairie Fire, and Lily's favorite, Damn Government.

While the business section was run-down and depressing, the residential section was quaint and well cared for. Neat little rows of brick and Austin stone houses lined either side of the street. A few people were working in their yards, mowing lawns, or planting spring flowers in the flower-beds. When they saw Stetson's truck, they stopped what they were doing and lifted their hands in greeting.

Everyone knew the Kingmans.

Stetson answered their greetings with a hand wave and a smile . . . until he pulled up to a four-way stop and the small postal truck sitting at the opposite corner beeped at him.

"Damn," he breathed under his breath. "Kitty

Carson."

Kitty Carson had been delivering the mail to the townsfolk of Cursed since Lily lived there. Although Kitty didn't just deliver the mail. She also delivered all the gossip in town—usually bad gossip. The more depressing the news, the more Kitty enjoyed relaying it. But she also had a kind heart. If someone got hurt or came down with a cold, she was the first person dropping off food. In the last few days, Lily had found brownies, sugar cookies, and a box of chocolate-covered cherries in Theo's mailbox.

The postal truck zipped up next to Stetson's truck. He sighed and rolled down the window. "Good mornin', Miss Kitty."

"Good mornin' yourself. Who you got in there with you, Stetson Kingman? You been hiding a girlfriend?" Kitty hopped out of the open door of her truck and leaned in Stetson's window. She had changed very little over the years. Her bright red hair was still cut at a razor-sharp angle along her pronounced jawline. She still had a bucktooth smile that lit up her face and Dolly Parton–sized boobs that made a shelf of her button-down postal uniform.

"Why if it isn't Lily Daltry!" she exclaimed. "I heard you were back in town helpin' your daddy. I would've rang the doorbell to say hi when I was delivering your mail, but I didn't want to impose on your daddy-daughter time."

Lily smiled and lifted a hand. "Hello, Ms. Carson."

"Like I've told you a million times, call me

Kitty, hon. Ms. Carson is my mama. And a meaner woman you'd never want to meet. She moved in with me last year and has made my life a living hell ever since." She glanced at Stetson. "But living in Cursed we're used to hell, ain't we? Speaking of hell, did you hear about poor Rita Rogers's boil? It showed up one morning right on the tip of her nose and made that pretty thang look just like Bozo the Clown." She shook her head. "What a cryin' shame, I tell you. Just a cryin' shame. But no more so than poor Sam Dickens, whose wife ran off with the UPS delivery guy. They even took the television Sam had ordered from Amazon. Now that's a cryin' shame. And did you hear about Mike Ledford—"

"I'm sorry, Miss Kitty," Stetson cut in. "But Lily has an appointment I need to get her to." He took his foot off the brake. "It was good talkin' with you."

As they took off from the stop sign, Lily glanced in the side mirror to see Kitty standing in the street watching them. "You didn't have to be so rude."

"Oh yes, I did. If I hadn't cut her off, we would've been there all day and those kids in Miss Vivian's class would never forgive me." Stetson pulled into the parking lot of the elementary school and stopped in front. "How long will you be?"

"It shouldn't take longer than a couple of hours."

Stetson nodded. "Then I'll pick you up around two thirty." When she started to get out, he stopped her. "Give Vivian and your daddy a chance, Lily. They both deserve to be happy."

She nodded before she slammed the door and headed into the school.

Vivian was waiting in her classroom.

"The kids are still at lunch," she said as she closed the door behind Lily. "But I'm glad you're here early. It will give us a chance to talk."

She led Lily over to the art table at the back of the room. As Lily sat down in the small chair, a flood of happy memories washed over her.

Vivian Fletcher had been the kind of teacher who made learning fun. She was vivacious and animated and wanted all her students to succeed. She'd looked past the shy, introverted little girl Lily had been and saw a creative child who needed an outlet for that creativity. Lily had written her first story in this classroom. Drawn her first fairy. Finally found her voice through writing and illustrating. And it was all due to Mrs. Fletcher. It was no wonder Lily's introverted father had fallen head over heels in love with her. Vivian had helped him find his voice too. Not to mention happiness.

"I'm so sorry, Lily," Vivian said as she sat down in the chair across from Lily. "I thought Theo had told you about us. No wonder you looked so surprised to see me at the cottage. And there I was running off at the mouth about me and your father being in love." She reached out and squeezed Lily's arm. "I didn't mean to spring something like that on you. You must've felt completely blindsided."

Lily had felt blindsided. But no more. She now realized Vivian was a perfect choice for her father. She would be the worst daughter ever if she didn't welcome Vivian into their family.

"I was a little surprised at first," she said. "But now I'm thrilled my father is going to marry my favorite teacher."

Tears came to Vivian's eyes, and she took Lily's hands in hers. "Thank you, Lily. I wouldn't marry your father without your blessing. I couldn't say it when you were in my class, but you were always my favorite student. And the most talented. I'm so proud of you and all you've accomplished. Your father told me that a toy company wants to turn your characters into dolls."

"I've been contacted, but I don't know if anything will come of it."

Vivian squeezed her hands. "Of course something will come of it. You just need to have faith." The bell rang, and she smiled. "Get ready for the stampede."

A few minutes later, sweaty children trickled into the classroom. They stared at Lily with wide eyes as they took their seats. Vivian wasted no time introducing her.

"Class, I'd like you to meet Lily Daltry. Like we talked about earlier, Lily was one of my students before she became a successful writer of the Fairy Prairie series. I expect you to give her a warm welcome and be on your best behavior."

The kids applauded enthusiastically as Lily stood. "It's a pleasure to be here. Mrs. Fletcher has told me that y'all have been writing stories, and I would love to hear some of them before I talk about mine."

The children took turns reading their stories. Lily knew immediately which kids were the shyest and which ones loved to be the center of attention. When they were finished reading, Lily talked about how she'd discovered her love of writing in Mrs. Fletcher's class and how she'd gone on to study writing and literature in college. Then she pulled a Fairy Prairie book from her tote bag. But before she started reading, the door opened. Stetson walked in.

"Excuse me." He pulled off his cowboy hat. "I thought you'd be done by now. I'll just come back—"

Vivian cut in. "Nonsense. Please stay, Mr. Kingman. The children have made thank you cards for your donation of the new playground sunshades. I know they'd love to present them to you once Miss Daltry is finished reading."

Stetson nodded and moved to the back where he leaned against the wall to wait. Lily didn't know why she suddenly felt so awkward and flustered. Her voice shook with nerves as she opened the book and started reading.

As always when she read her books out loud, she used the voices she heard in her head. Daffodil's voice was brassy and loud. Apple's voice was soft and sweet. Whippoorwill had a rich, charming voice. Barley spoke excitedly and fast. And Beetlebub spoke in a deep growl. Poppy didn't speak. At least not with her voice. She spoke with a feather dipped in whatever was handy—red berry juice, yellow flower pollen, and dark soil. She spoke with her writing and her pictures.

"But why can't Poppy talk?" A girl with freckles and glasses asked after Lily had finished reading the story. It was a question a lot of kids asked at Lily's book readings.

"Because she doesn't want to," Lily replied. "She'd rather express herself through her drawings and writing."

"But speaking would be so much easier," the boy next to the freckled girl said. "Drawing and writing take a long time."

"True," Lily said. "And maybe one day, when she's ready, Poppy will speak."

"In the next book?" a girl in a bright-pink hoodie with a crooked ponytail asked.

Lily wished she could answer. But she didn't have a clue what was going to happen in the next Fairy Prairie book. "Maybe," she said. "You'll have to read the next one to find out." If there was a next one.

"When Poppy does talk," the hoodie girl continued. "I hope she tells Beetlebub to go to H-E-double-hockey-sticks."

The entire class laughed, and Lily couldn't help glancing at Stetson.

She'd done a good job of making Beetlebub the villain of Fairy Prairie and the most disliked fairy in the country—if not the world. Her mother's stories always had happy fairies living happy lives. Lily was the one who added the villain. And not just any villain, but a villain she knew well.

Stetson Kingman.

Lily had loved making him the evil fairy ... and then giving him his just deserts by having him fall off his dragonfly into a mud puddle or get hit in the face with an overripe blueberry or shot with a needle sharp thorn.

Stetson falling in the garden and getting stuck with rose thorns had been life imitating fiction. Except he hadn't acted like a big ol' bully. He'd actually been quite nice.

As he had been on the drive into town.

His dark gaze locked with hers, and she suddenly felt . . . connected. Like there was this invisible line between them and Stetson was reeling it in, pulling her closer and closer.

Without looking away from Stetson's warm brown eyes, she answered the little girl. "Maybe there's a reason Beetlebub is so grumpy. Maybe he just needs a friend."

# CHAPTER EIGHT

"WHAT ABOUT SETH?" GAGE SAT in the chair in front of Stetson's desk. "You embarrassed him pretty badly when you reamed him out for coming into the arena when you were working with Fancy Dancer."

Stetson continued to pace behind the desk. "I can't believe he'd want revenge on me for protecting him from getting his ass trampled. Besides, he loves animals too much to be behind the mutilation."

Gage lifted an eyebrow. "Every employee on this ranch has you convinced they love animals, Boss. Otherwise they wouldn't have a job."

"But Seth doesn't have the security code to the stables."

"No, but he could've easily watched one of us enter it. It's not like we've been careful around the ranch workers. We didn't think it was one of us causing all the trouble."

No, Stetson had never considered it might be one of his people—someone he trusted and thought of as part of the Kingman Ranch family. He clenched his fists and turned to the window.

"Fine. Then keep Seth on the list. What does that give us for total possible culprits?"

"Twenty-two who are directly connected to the horses and stables. Fifty-three if we include the alfalfa farmers, cattle cowboys, and the people who work at the house."

Stetson blew out his breath and turned to Gage. "So basically it could be anyone."

"Pretty much. I saw just the one person moving toward the stables the other night, but they could be working for someone. Have you considered your stepmother?"

Just the mention of Delilah Kingman had Stetson tensing. "Delilah wasn't married to my father long enough to be considered a stepmother. Daddy went to Vegas for a stock show and came back with two horses and Delilah. He died from a heart attack two weeks later. Thankfully, he had her sign a prenuptial agreement that gave his children control of the ranch in the event of his death."

"Which is my point. It sounded like she was pretty pissed off she didn't get anything."

"She got something. She got a hefty check from his life insurance policy. Enough to buy herself a big mansion in Dallas. And from what I hear, she found herself another wealthy husband."

"Just want to make sure we cover all the bases, Boss."

Stetson nodded. "And I appreciate it. If they're daring enough to physically knock a man out, that's too daring. We need to catch the guy before someone else gets hurt."

"Why do you assume it's a man?"

Stetson and Gage turned to the doorway. Adeline stood there, looking much too thin and pale. As if a strong wind would carry her away like scattered dandelion seeds.

"It could be a woman," she said as she moved into the room. "We have numerous female employees." She glanced at Gage. "Hello, Mr. Reardon."

Gage became mute whenever he was around Adeline. Instead of answering, he picked up his beat-up cowboy hat he'd tossed on the chair next to him and got to his feet. "I'll just get back to work, Boss, and let you talk to your sister."

When he was gone, Stetson laughed. "How does it feel to make men speechless with your beauty, Addie?"

She took the chair Gage had vacated and ignored the question. "How's Tab?"

Stetson sat down in the chair behind the desk. "Doc stitched him up and he's staying at his sister's in town for a few days so she can keep an eye on him. I stopped by to see him this afternoon and he seems fine."

Addie rolled her eyes. "Doc is the ranch veterinarian, Stetson. Tab should see an MD."

"Doc has stitched up a lot of ranch hands over the years, Addie—all of us Kingmans included. I trust Doc to know if Tab needs to go to the county hospital. And I'd just as soon keep the details of what happened from becoming fodder for Cursed gossip hounds."

She sighed. "So we're still not calling in the

sheriff?"

"Not yet."

"But if you do find the man—or woman—who's causing all the trouble, you'll call the sheriff then, right?" When he didn't answer right away, she leaned forward in her chair. "This isn't the Old West, Stet. We're not going to deal out our own justice."

"I'll call the sheriff." It wasn't a lie. Stetson planned to hand the asshole over to the law—after he dealt out a little Kingman justice of his own. "Have any luck finding a new housekeeper?"

"I'm afraid not."

"What about promoting one of the maids?"

"I already asked, but none of them want the longer hours or to have to live here with the wild Kingmans." She got up. "And I can't say I blame them. I'm going to try looking outside of the county and see if I have any better luck."

After Adeline left, Stetson went back over the list of his employees. Few ranches did background checks. Experienced ranch workers were hard to come by. If someone was willing to work, Stetson hired them. If they caused problems, he fired them. He didn't even know much about Gage. Gage didn't talk about his past. But Stetson didn't need to know about a man's past to know if he was trustworthy. Gage had proven himself worthy time and time again. So had most of the other hands who had been on the ranch for years.

Frustrated, Stetson closed his laptop and headed to the stables. Instead of working with one of the horses, he saddled up Rooster and rode out. Riding the ranch had always calmed him.

The Kingman Ranch had started out as a cattle ranch. But Stetson's grandfather had been a firm believer that you shouldn't keep all your eggs in one basket. After King inherited the ranch, he quickly bought out his brother Jack and added thoroughbred horse breeding and farming to the family business. The ranch profits grew. Especially when oil was found. More money made King even hungrier for it. But if the ranch was to continue to grow, King had needed more land. When he found out the neighboring rancher's daughter was the same age as his only son, he knew he had a way to get that land.

Stetson's father and mother were married the summer after they graduated from college. Grandpa Cutler had never been much of a rancher, and he was happy to hand over the reins to his new son-in-law. Although it was really King who was running things. With the addition of the Cutler Ranch, the Kingman Ranch became one of the biggest ranches in Texas. To make sure everyone knew it, King built his huge monstrosity of a castle where he could hold court.

Unfortunately, King didn't get to enjoy the castle he built for long. Only three years after finishing the stone mansion, he died of a heart attack—a year after bringing in a gardener to create an English garden.

Although it had turned out to be Gwen who was the genius behind Theo's success as a gardener. She was the one who designed the garden fit for a king . . . and then she'd enticed the King's son. Leaving King's poor daughter-in-law with a broken heart.

And his grandson hating the woman who was responsible.

As a kid, it had been so easy to let that hate spill over onto Gwen's daughter. To blame her for the sins of her mother. As an adult, Stetson had still felt resentful towards Lily. The way she'd ignored Theo hadn't helped. But in the last week, he'd realized he was wrong. Lily wasn't her mother. Nor was she a spoiled, selfish author. It was obvious she cared about Theo. And children. Watching her interact with Vivian's class was like watching a butterfly come out of its cocoon. Shy Lily had turned into an animated, laughing woman . . . who had completely captivated Stetson.

"Hey, Bubba!"

He slowed his horse and turned to see Delaney riding up. It was hard not to admire the way his sister sat a saddle. No one rode like Del. Not even Buck, who prided himself on being an excellent horseman. She didn't have to pull up on the reins to get the horse to slow. She trained her cutting horses using leg cues. With just the pressure of her knees and heels she could get her horses to do just about anything she wanted them to. Stetson was proud as hell of his sister.

"Hey, Del. What are you doing out here?"

"I was coming back from checking on my goats," she said. "I've got a new kid! I thought GoGo had a few weeks before her due date, but she dropped early. Dudley is about the cutest thing you've ever seen in your life."

Stetson laughed. "You say that about every newborn animal. Another kid? Doesn't that make five this season? Before long we're going to become goat herders."

Del tipped up her chin. "And what's wrong with that?"

"Not a thing as long as you're the one making sure they're taken care of. I already have enough on my plate."

"Whose fault is that? You have four siblings who are more than capable of helping you out. But you let Buck and Wolfe run wild. You let Addie stay in her tower. And besides caring for my goats, you never expect me to do anything around the ranch."

"And yet you do. You work harder than most of my ranch hands."

"Because this is my ranch too, Stet. I love it as much as I love my stubborn brother who is going to work himself into an early grave like granddaddy and daddy if he doesn't learn how to delegate!"

He would've laughed at her tirade—his sister was cute when she got ticked—if he hadn't read the concern in her blue eyes. She'd not only lost her mother when she was only a toddler, she'd also lost her father when she was only thirteen. Technically, she'd become an orphan. An orphan raised by her inept big brother. She didn't want to lose anyone else. He couldn't blame her.

Stetson reached out and tugged on one of the braids she always wore.

"I'm not going anywhere, Delly Belly. But if

it will make you feel better, I'll delegate more to Buck and Wolfe. You're right. I have been letting them run a little wild. But Addie has been through a lot. She needs some time to get over her grief."

"I disagree," Delaney said. "What she needs is something to take her mind off Danny's death."

"I don't think anything is going to do that."

Delaney sighed. "You're probably right. She and Danny were joined at the hip since they were kids. She must feel like a piece of her is gone. Still, I don't think hiding away in her tower is going to help. Like you, she needs to get out. Have a little fun. It's Taco Tuesday at Nasty Jack's. We should get Addie to go. She loves tacos—at least she used to."

"I think that's a great idea. I'm sure you, Wolfe, and Buck can talk her into going with y'all."

"We've already tried to get her to go to Jack's with us. She flat out refuses." Delaney paused and shot him a look. "But if I told her you won't go unless she does, she might do it. She's been real worried about you working so much."

"I can't go. Someone needs to stay here to keep an eye on things."

"Gage can do that. I'm sure he'll call if there's a problem. You need a break from thinking about the ranch as much as Addie needs one from thinking about Danny. Besides, it's been a long time since the Kingmans have gone to Jack's and raised a little hell."

"There's a reason for that," Stetson said. "Last time, Wolfe and Buck got into it with a couple of drifters, and I had to pay for two cases of broken glasses and a busted barstool."

Delaney sent him her wide-eyed pleading look. The one he'd always found hard to resist. "Pretty please, Bubba."

Later that night, Stetson found himself standing at the long bar at Nasty Jack's nursing a bottle of Coors Light while Buck and Delaney argued over what Texas baseball team would make it to the World Series. Addie had pleaded a headache and hadn't come. And Wolfe had yet to arrive. He and Buck had wanted to drive separately—no doubt because they were both hoping to pick up a girl at the bar.

There were quite a few to choose from. Nasty Jack's was packed. Besides the Kingman Ranch, the bar was the most successful business in Cursed. Of course, some would say that the business was still part of the Kingman dynasty. Stetson's great uncle Jack Kingman owned the bar. He was close to eighty now, but still showed up every night to keep an eye on things. Stetson might've joined him at the table in the corner where he always sat if Jack hadn't been such a grumpy old dude.

The bar was appropriately named.

Jack's grandson, Jasper, who ran the bar, was the complete opposite. He always had a smile on his face. "How you doin', cuz? Can I get you another beer?"

"I'm good." As soon as he finished this one, he was heading home. Nasty Jack's had never been his thing.

"Did you finish getting the spring branding done?" Jasper asked.

"Almost. Thanks again for helping out."

Jasper nodded as he wiped off the bar. "No problem. I always enjoy spending time at the ranch."

"You're always welcome." He downed the last of his beer and set the bottle on the bar. "And now I think I'll head on—"

"My, my. If it isn't Stetson Kingman himself."

Stetson turned to see Lorelei Cordell standing there with a slight smirk on her red painted lips. He had gone to school with Lorelei. His best friend had dated her best friend, which had thrown Stetson and Lorelei together on more than a few occasions. But besides a drunken make-out session, he'd never been interested in her. And she'd never been interested in him . . . until after her second divorce. Now every time he came to town, she popped up out of nowhere. It was kinda spooky.

"Hey, Lorelei. How are you?"

She sent him a seductive smile, revealing a smudge of red lipstick on her front tooth. "I've been told mighty fine."

Not knowing how to reply to that, he moved on. "How are your kids?"

"They're ornery as ever. You were smart to skip the kids." She held up her half-empty margarita. "They'll drive you to drink." She drained the glass of everything but the rim of salt before setting it down on the bar. "Do you want to dance?"

Stetson shook his head. "I'm not really much of a dancer. I just stopped by for a beer with my family."

Lorelei glanced over at Delaney and Buck, who were still arguing. "I'm sure they won't mind if you dance with me." She grabbed his hand and tugged him toward the crowded dance floor. "I promise to take it easy on you."

Lorelei's idea of taking it easy was plastering her body to his and gyrating her hips. "How's this?" she asked. "Is it slow enough for you?"

Seeing as how the song was a fast polka, it was too slow. But he kept his thoughts to himself and hoped the song would end quickly. When it did, Lorelei continued to hang on him like a squashed bug on a windshield.

"Just one more," she pleaded. "I love this song."

Stetson started to decline and unpeel himself when a couple moving onto the dance floor caught his attention. Wolfe flashed him a wide grin before he pulled Lily into his arms and two-stepped her away.

Before Stetson could even get his mouth closed, they came back around.

"Hey, big bro!" Wolfe called.

Lily's green-eyed gaze locked with Stetson's for a second before Wolfe spun her, her short skirt twirling around toned legs, then danced her off into the crowd.

"I know you don't dance, but you could at least move your feet."

Lorelei's words made Stetson realize he was just standing there . . . waiting for Wolfe and Lily to come back around. When they did, he stopped Wolfe and pulled him close so the two women wouldn't overhear.

"What are you doing?"

"Last time I checked, it's called the two-step," Wolfe said.

"You know what I mean."

Wolfe shrugged. "If you aren't going to make a move, big brother, I will."

Stetson clenched his teeth. "Fine. I'll make a move if you back off."

Wolfe flashed him a satisfied cat-who-ate-the-canary smile before he turned to Lily. "I'm sorry, Lily, but I think I pulled something on that last spin. Do you mind if Stetson finishes the dance?"

"Wait one doggone minute," Lorelei said. "I was dancing with—" She cut off when Wolfe hooked an arm around her waist and sent her a slow smile.

"Now, Lorelei, I'm sure you don't mind helping an injured man back to his truck?"

"You poor thing," Lorelei cooed. "Of course I'll help you to your truck. In fact, if you want, you can come over to my house. My second husband, Rodney, had back problems and only my massages could get out all his kinks."

Wolfe grinned. "I don't know, honey. I've got a lot of kinks. But I'm willing to give it a try if you are." As he ushered Lorelei off the dance floor, he glanced over his shoulder at Stetson. "Now y'all don't have too much fun without me, ya hear?"

# CHAPTER NINE

EIGHT YEARS AGO, LILY WOULD'VE been devastated by Wolfe's rejection. Now she only found it humorous. "It looks like I've been ditched for a better prospect."

Stetson didn't seem to find the humor in the situation. "What are you doing here with Wolfe?"

"He stopped by the cottage to check on my father and asked me if I wanted to come dancing. Since Vivian was there for dinner, and I felt a little like a third wheel, I accepted. Do you have a problem with that?"

Before Stetson could answer, a two-stepping couple bumped into her from behind, knocking her off balance. Stetson reached out to steady her, his strong fingers settling on her waist.

Heat flashed through Lily. The day she'd read to Vivian's class, she'd felt a strange connection to Stetson. She thought it had to do with their growing friendship. But the feeling that washed through her at his touch had nothing to do with friendship and everything to do with him being a man and her being a woman. It wasn't just a tingle of sexual awareness, it was an entire tidal wave.

When she grabbed onto his arms for balance and felt the flex of his biceps, the wave threatened to take her under.

"You okay?" he asked.

No. She wasn't okay. She wasn't okay at all. She was fine with liking Stetson as a friend. She was not okay with desiring him. She looked around for Wolfe so she could ask him to take her home. But before she could find him, the song changed and Stetson drew her into his arms.

"We better dance before we get trampled."

As they joined the other dancers, she tried to focus on Stetson's face and not on the feel of his hand on her waist or his muscles beneath her fingers. But even his features made her feel overheated. The warm amber flecks in his dark eyes. The sexy scruff on his strong jaw. The plump curve of his bottom lip. What was the matter with her? It had to be the margarita Wolfe had bought her before he'd led her out to the dance floor. She was just buzzed. That was all.

It made sense. As Stetson expertly waltzed her around the floor, she felt lightheaded and breathless. Like she had stepped onto a whirling carnival ride. Everything blurred around her . . . except for the hypnotic pull of Stetson's dark gaze. And the flex of his broad shoulders beneath her palm. And the tightening of his hands on her fingers and waist.

Trying to find her balance, she pulled her gaze away from his and started a conversation—anything to take her mind off the physical reaction she was having to him. "I didn't think you knew how to dance."

"Why would you think that?"

"Because you never danced at any of your family's parties. Not even your own high school graduation party."

"You were at my high school graduation party?"

"Not exactly. My mom wouldn't let me attend. She didn't want her middle school-age daughter learning bad things from wild high schoolers. So I watched the garden party from my attic. You didn't dance once. But you did make out with Stella Fremont behind the lilac bushes."

Stetson laughed. She knew she had heard him laugh before, but she couldn't remember when. Nor did she remember it being so deep and seductive.

"Why, you little spy," he teased. "What else did you see?"

She tried to keep her focus on their conversation and not the scent of rugged man that filled her lungs with every inhale. "I saw Addie and Danny sneak off to the barn and Wolfe get in trouble with my father for stealing beers out of the adults' cooler." She paused. "And at the end of the night, I saw you get in an argument with your daddy. I couldn't hear what you said, but it looked like you were pretty mad. You always seemed to be mad at your father. Why? Especially that night when he'd thrown you a graduation party and given you a brand-new truck."

It took him a long time to answer. When he did, his voice held no remnant of laughter. "Like you and Theo, my father and I always had a communication problem. But we fought rather than kept silent." He paused. "Something I regret."

"We all have regrets, Stetson. I regret not being a better daughter to Theo."

"But you have a chance to rectify that."

It was true. Stetson had no chance. His father was gone. Maybe that explained why he still drove the truck his father had given him.

The song ended and another waltz began. She expected Stetson to release her. Instead, he drew her closer and kept dancing.

"I remember your high school graduation party too," he said.

"Of course you do. I was a complete idiot that night."

"You weren't an idiot. You were just a young girl with a major crush who happened to get the wrong room."

She lifted her gaze to his. "That's not what you said that night. You gave me a scalding lecture about how stupid my actions were and how disappointed my father would be if he ever found out."

He cringed. "Okay, so I might've overreacted. I've never been good with surprises. And climbing into bed and finding you naked was surprising."

She giggled. "You yelped like a startled dog when I reached out and touched you."

"I did not yelp."

"You did too. You yelped and jumped out of bed so quickly your feet got tangled in the sheets and you landed on the floor." Her giggles turned into laughter as he continued to waltz her around the floor. "I wish I could've taken a picture of your face when you finally turned on the lights. It was priceless."

He laughed too. "You should talk. When you saw me, you looked like you'd seen a ghost."

"I *was* shocked. I was expecting the Kingman prince and instead got the Kingman beast." As soon as the words were out, she wanted them back. But it was too late. They hung there like a dense, cruel fog. Stetson's smile faded, and he stopped dancing and released her.

"I bet that was a surprise. Thanks for the dance, Lillian Leigh." He turned and walked away.

She tried to go after him, but the song changed to a line dance and people flooded the floor. By the time she pushed her way through the crowd, Stetson was nowhere to be found. Neither was Wolfe. He'd probably gone home with Lorelei.

Luckily, she found Delaney and Buck at the bar. Delaney had had too much to drink and rambled the entire drive back to the ranch about the new foal and baby goat and how cute Jasper was and if it was wrong to kiss a cousin. Lily listened with half an ear. Her mind was too wrapped up in hurting Stetson's feelings. He'd been much crueler to her in the past, but that didn't give her the right to be cruel to him now.

"I just don't get it," Delaney broke into Lily's thoughts. "They are the complete opposites. He's big, gruff, and bossy and she's this quiet little mouse that—"

Buck cut in. "Shut up, Del. You're drunk and talking stupid."

"I'm not stupid." Delaney slugged Buck. He slugged her back, and she shoved him, causing the truck to swerve into the other lane, narrowly missing an oncoming car.

Terrified, Lily yelled at the top of her lungs. "That's enough!"

Delaney and Buck stopped fighting and turned to her. She pointed at Buck. "Stop antagonizing your sister and watch where you're going before you get us all killed." She pointed at Delaney. "And Del, stop distracting your brother while he's driving and shut up. You're drunk."

They both exchanged looks before they did exactly what she said. A few minutes later, she heard Delaney mutter under her breath something that sounded like, "Maybe they do fit together."

When they got to the ranch, Buck dropped her off at the cottage. Lily only went in long enough to make sure her father was sleeping soundly before she slipped out the back door and headed down the path that led to the Kingman castle. Like the first night she'd arrived, the kitchen was dark except for the flickering firelight coming from the great room. When she went to cross the foyer, she heard Buck and Delaney arguing as they climbed the stairs. She held back until they were gone, then followed the flickering light.

Stetson sat in King's chair by the fire. He'd taken off his hat and cowboy boots, and his stocking feet were propped up on the fireplace hearth. A book lay open on his lap, but he wasn't reading it. He was sipping amber liquid from the glass he held and staring at the flames.

Lily stopped in the doorway, unsure of how to go about apologizing. Before she could find the words, he glanced up.

She slowly lifted a hand. "Hey."

He turned back to the fire. Obviously, he wasn't going to make this easy.

She moved closer. "What are you reading?"

He glanced down at the book as if he'd forgotten it was there. "A book about the battle of Waterloo."

"Interesting."

He arched a brow at her. "A little more intense than fairies."

"True, but not nearly as entertaining." She sat down in the chair next to his. "I'm sorry. What I said was cruel. But you have to admit you were rather beastly to me when we were growing up. You hated me."

He looked down at the amber liquid in his glass. "I didn't hate you."

"You didn't like me. And I could never figure out what I'd done to you."

He swirled the whiskey. "Nothing. You didn't do anything. You were just an easy target for my anger."

"I don't understand. What did you have to be angry about? You were a Kingman. You had everything."

He drained the glass and set it down on the table next to him. "Not everything. I didn't have my mother."

She rested her head back on the chair and

released her breath. "I was angry after my mother died too. Angry at God for taking her. Angry at her for leaving me. And angry at my dad for not seeing she was sick sooner and getting her help. Maybe I'm still angry at Daddy. Maybe that's why I didn't come home sooner." Instead, she had stayed in England and sulked. Maybe if she'd come home and addressed her anger, she could have moved on from her grief sooner and she wouldn't be this emotionally stunted woman without any life outside her imaginary fairy world.

"Your father couldn't have known your mom had cancer."

She rolled her head and glanced over at him. "And your father couldn't have stopped your mother from getting in the car accident. But that's why you were so angry at him, wasn't it? You blamed him for your mom's death."

There was a long stretch of silence before Stetson spoke. "He was to blame."

Lily lifted her head and stared at him. "How was he to blame for your mother's car sliding on the ice and hitting that tree? He wasn't even in the car with her."

He stared at the flames of the fire. "But his hateful words were. Which was why she was driving so fast the night of the accident. Why she didn't take the time to put on her seatbelt."

"I don't understand."

He got up and stood in front of the fireplace with his back to her. "My daddy didn't love my mama. He never loved her."

"How do you know that?"

He paused before he spoke in a low voice. "Because I overheard him flat out tell her that on the night she died—tell her that he'd only married her because his father wanted her land."

Lily was stunned. She would've been devastated if she'd overheard her father telling her mother that. As a child, her entire sense of security had been wrapped around her parents' love for her. And each other. To have that security shattered, and on the same night you lost your mother, must've been almost too much to bear. And yet, Stetson had borne it.

"I'm so sorry," she said. "That must've been awful for you to overhear. But sometimes people say things in anger that they don't really mean."

"He meant it. He was in love with another woman. My mother found out. That's why they were arguing."

"Oh my God." Lily covered her mouth as tears welled in her eyes.

"So now you know why I'm a beast instead of a prince," Stetson said. "And since I'm drunk and feeling pretty beastly right now, it might be best if you go back to the cottage, Lily."

She should have. She should have gotten up and left. If Stetson needed comforting, his siblings were there to do it. Except she would almost bet he hadn't told his siblings about what he'd over-heard that night. He had always been protective of his brothers and sisters. He wouldn't have wanted them to be as hurt as he'd been. Lily had to wonder if he'd shared his burden with anyone else.

If not, then why her?

That one question kept her from leaving. She got up and walked over to where Stetson stood. She didn't say anything. There wasn't anything to say. No words could make that kind of hurt better. So instead of offering comfort with empty words, she moved behind him and wrapped her arms around his waist.

He stiffened, and she waited for him to pull away. But he didn't. He just stood there facing the fire as she pressed her cheek against his back and let her tears soak into the soft cotton of his Western shirt.

But this time, she wasn't crying because of something Stetson said.

This time, she cried for him.

# CHAPTER TEN

STETSON COULDN'T REMEMBER THE LAST time he'd been held. Not just hugged— but actually held. His siblings gave him hugs all the time. Delaney could break a bone with her tight hugs. Adeline's were much softer. And his brothers gave him the quick man hugs that were always accompanied by a hard thump on the back. But no one, not even the women he had gone to bed with over the years, had held him the way Lily was doing.

Being held was one of those things you didn't know you needed until you were locked in someone's arms.

His mother had probably been the last person to hold him. After her death, Stetson had gone without the comfort. Some of the fault was his. His mother's tragic death and the events leading up to it had ripped his heart in two. To survive, he'd allowed his heart to harden and he became the type of person who didn't let anyone get too close. Not even his family.

And yet, he'd let Lily in. He'd shared with her something he hadn't even shared with his siblings.

Of course, he hadn't told her the entire truth. He hadn't told her the woman his father had been having an affair with was her mother.

And he wouldn't.

He couldn't bring himself to ruin the good memories she had of her mom. But even sharing half his secret felt good. Like he'd lanced a wound and released the poison festering inside.

Lily's arms were the healing salve.

He knew he was a little drunk and tomorrow would regret opening up to her. But for now, he didn't regret it. For now, he wanted to remain right where he was: held tightly in Lily's arms with her petite body pressed to his. He didn't know how long they stood there. The flames of the fire had almost burned out when he noticed the damp spot on the back of his shirt.

"Lily? Are you crying?"

She didn't answer right away. When she did, her voice was clogged with tears. "No." He went to turn around, but her arms tightened. "Okay, so I'm crying. But you know I'm a crybaby."

She *had* cried a lot as a kid, but he'd given her good cause. He slipped a hand over her hands clasped around his waist and rubbed his thumb along her knuckles. She had the softest skin. It was like the petals of a rose.

"No you aren't," he said. "You didn't cry once when you were eight and fell off your bike in the gravel driveway and scraped both your knees."

"I started to, but then you came charging out of nowhere and scooped me up in your arms and scared the tears right back into their ducts."

He chuckled. "And here I thought you'd gotten the wind knocked out of you and couldn't talk. You didn't say a word the entire time I bandaged your knees."

She turned her head, resting her forehead on the spot between his shoulder blades. "I'd forgotten about you cleaning my scrapes and putting princess Band-Aids on my knees." She laughed, her soft breath warming the damp spot on his shirt. "I never took you for a princess Band-Aid guy."

"Hey, I have little sisters. I got used to princess everything."

There was a slight hesitation before she spoke again. "You were a good big brother."

"But a bullying beast to you."

"I survived. I just learned to stay away from you."

She wasn't staying away from him now. She was pressed against his back and seemed in no hurry to leave. He wasn't in any hurry for her to leave either. He didn't know if it was the alcohol or the hypnotic glowing embers of the fire. Or even a spell cast by angry fairies for destroying their garden. All he knew was he didn't want to move from this spot.

"Was my bullying one of the reasons you left the ranch and didn't come back?" he asked as he continued to trace his fingertips over the soft skin of her hands.

"No. Mostly I left because of my mother. The memories were too painful. We were very close . . . maybe too close."

He remembered how close Lily and Gwen had been. He had been jealous of their closeness. Jealous he could never again experience that closeness with his mother. That was probably just another reason he'd picked on Lily.

"I'm sorry about your mom," he said. He felt the sudden change in Lily's body. The loosening of her arms. The drawing away. He wanted to hold onto her, but he knew he couldn't. He released her hands and turned.

Her cheeks were flushed and her eyes still held a few tears, turning the green to sparkling emerald. She had never looked more beautiful.

"I should probably go check on my father," she said.

He needed to say something. Anything. But his brain seemed sluggish. He had talked so easily while she held him. Now he had no words. When he didn't speak, she took a step back.

"Well, goodnight, Stetson." She turned to leave, but he stepped in front of her. She lifted her eyes to him in question. But he didn't have an answer. He didn't know why he'd stopped her.

Or maybe he did.

He lowered his head and kissed her. Not a deep kiss. Just a light brush of heated lips against heated lips. And yet, the brief touch was like a bolt of lightning spiking through him. Electric. Shocking. He drew back and stared at her. She stared at him with the same stunned confusion. Then as if the electricity of the kiss had magnetized them, they came back together.

This time, it wasn't a mere brush. This time,

their lips fed with a hungry madness. Stetson wanted like he had never wanted before. He wanted her full lips and her wet mouth and her hot tongue and her nipping teeth. He wanted the soft breasts pressed against him and the curvy hips that wiggled closer. But before Stetson could get everything he wanted, they were interrupted.

"Oops," Wolfe said. "I didn't realize we had company."

Stetson and Lily pulled apart as quickly as they had come together. They stood there staring at each other, their breathing harsh and loud. He didn't know what she was thinking, but he knew what he was.

What the hell had just happened?

Wolfe cleared his throat. "If you'll excuse me, I'll just let you get back to . . . ."

Lily blinked and then shook her head as if to clear it. Stetson knew how she felt. But shaking his head didn't clear the emotions rioting inside him. He had been completely blindsided by the intensity of their kiss. He wanted to pull her back for another. And another. And another.

"No, it's fine, Wolfe," Lily said as she tugged down the shirt he had started to lift when Wolfe arrived. "I was just leaving." Without a word to Stetson, she walked out of the room.

Wolfe waited for the sound of the back door closing before he grinned at Stetson. "Sorry, bro." He flopped down in a chair. "I didn't realize you were planning on having sex with Lily on the couch in the great room. Next time, I would suggest the privacy of your bedroom."

Hoping more alcohol would soothe his rioting emotions, Stetson took his glass over to the bar to pour himself another whiskey. "We weren't going to have sex. It was just a kiss."

Wolfe laughed. "If that was just a kiss, then she must be damn good between the sheets."

Stetson whirled around, spilling half the whiskey he'd just poured. "Shut the fuck up, Wolfe!"

Wolfe drew back in surprise. "Easy, bro. I was just making an observation. "I'm not after Lily. She's all yours."

"She's not mine. Lily's not some prize to claim." Stetson took a deep swallow of whiskey.

Wolfe leaned forward. "Wait a minute, don't tell me that you're not going to pursue her. From what I could tell by that kiss, she likes you as much as you like her. So why not enjoy each other while she's here?"

"Because she's not the sophisticated woman we thought she was. She's the same shy, introverted Lily we grew up with. And I don't want her hurt."

Wolfe studied him for a long moment. "Are you sure you're worried about Lily getting hurt and not yourself?"

It was a good question. One he didn't have an answer to. Whatever had taken place tonight was much more than he'd been prepared for. Lily had stripped him of the protective armor he'd worn for most his life, leaving him exposed. And scared. Stetson didn't like feeling either of those emotions. He'd felt them the night of his mother's accident and sworn he would never feel them again.

He tossed down the rest of his whiskey and set the glass on the bar. "I'm not going to get hurt. And neither is Lily. Because I'm going to stay away from her. The kiss was a mistake. One that won't be repeated."

Wolfe rolled to his feet. "Then you won't mind if I take a shot at—" He didn't get to finish before Stetson grabbed him by the shirt and shoved him up against the wall. Wolfe looked completely stunned. Stetson had never gotten physical with his brothers. His job was to protect them. But now all he could think about was protecting Lily.

"You will stay away from Lily, Wolfe. Do I make myself clear?"

Wolfe's eyes narrowed for a fraction of a second before a smile spread across his face. "Sure, Stet. You've made yourself perfectly clear. But I can't guarantee Buck will heed the warning if he finds out you're not in the hunt."

"Then don't tell him." Stetson released his brother. "Now I'm going to bed."

But once he climbed into bed, Stetson couldn't sleep.

The kiss he'd shared with Lily kept playing over and over again in his head. If she'd been any other woman, he might be willing to investigate his strong reaction to her. But Lily wasn't just a woman. She was Theo's daughter. She was also Stetson's father's mistress's daughter.

That made things way too complicated.

Stetson finally fell asleep in the wee hours of the morning. He woke to the sun shining in through his window. He never woke to the sun.

It was always still dark when he got out of bed. He quickly showered and got dressed. As he was hurrying down the stairs, he didn't see the bucket until it was too late. He tripped over it and would've gone tumbling down with the bucket if he hadn't caught himself on the banister. He sat down hard and banged his tailbone on the stairs.

"What the hell!" he bellowed. "Who put that bucket there?"

A woman Stetson had never seen before appeared from around the curve of the stairway holding a mop. She had strawberry-blond hair that hung down her back in a long braid and a surprised look on her round, freckled face.

"Oh! I'm so sorry, sir," she said with a thick southern accent. "I didn't think anyone was still upstairs in bed." She quickly climbed the stairs. "Here, let me help ya up." She bent over and the mop handle cracked him in the head. "Oops!" She dropped the mop and went to help him again, but her feet slipped on the wet stairs. He grabbed her before she took a tumble and she landed in his lap just as Lily came out of the kitchen.

Why he should feel guilty, he didn't know. But damned if his face didn't fill with heat when she glanced up and saw them.

"I fell," he said lamely.

Lily's eyes turned as frosty as late winter grass. "I bet it's hard walking down the stairs with a woman in your arms."

"Oh, he wasn't carryin' me down the stairs," the woman said. "It would take at least three men to do that. He fell over my bucket and then, klutz that I am, I fell on top of him trying to help him up."

Lily's eyebrows arched. "Who are you?"

It was a good question. One Stetson would've asked if he'd had his full wits about him. During his shower, he'd convinced himself that his reaction to Lily the night before had to do with too much alcohol. But he wasn't drunk this morning, and just the sight of her had his heart thumping so fast it felt like it would hop out of his chest.

"Lily!" Adeline came around the corner and gave Lily a hug. "It's so good to see you. I'm sorry I haven't been over to the cottage to say hello. I've become a little bit of a homebody since . . ." She let the sentence trail off.

"I understand," Lily said. "I was so sorry to hear about Danny."

Adeline nodded and was about to say something when she glanced up the stairs. "What in the world is going on?"

"It was all my fault, Miss Kingman," the woman on Stetson's lap said. "I left a bucket on the stairs and this here gentleman tripped over it. When I tried to help him up, I fell on top of him—which I'm sure almost crushed the life right out of him. He still looks a little stunned." She tapped him on the cheek none-too-gently. "You okay, sir?"

He stared at her. "Could you get off me?"

"Oh! Of course." She got to her feet and would've slipped again if Stetson hadn't reached out and steadied her. She flashed him a bright smile. "Thank you kindly. Like I said before, I'm a bit of a klutz." She glanced down at Adeline. "But a great housekeeper. I promise, Miss Kingman."

Adeline smiled weakly. "I'm sure you will be. This is my brother Stetson Kingman, and our good friend Lily Daltry. Stetson and Lily, this is our new housekeeper, Gretchen Flaherty."

Gretchen's eyes widened as she watched Stetson get to his feet. "You're the big boss? Oh, I'm so sorry, sir. I'll get this mess cleaned up right away." She picked up the mop and started mopping up whatever cleaning solution had spilled out of the bucket as Stetson gingerly made his way down to Adeline and Lily.

They both looked like they were about to burst out laughing.

He scowled. "Just what's so amusing? I could've broken my neck." He glanced at Gretchen and kept his voice low so she couldn't hear. "I take it she was the only applicant."

Adeline nodded. "But I like her. She's enthusiastic. I tried to explain that the part-time maids will do most of the cleaning and all she needs to do is supervise. But she says that her mama taught her that idle hands are the devil's workshop."

He snorted. "Let's hope her enthusiasm doesn't get one of us killed."

"I think our family can survive." She looked at Lily. "What brings you to the house, Lily? I hope your father is all right."

"He's doing much better, thank you. He only takes the painkillers at night and has started using his crutches." She glanced at Stetson. "I just stopped by to talk to Stetson. If you have time."

Stetson didn't want to talk to Lily. He wanted

to stay completely away from her and the feelings she seemed to evoke. Just standing near her made him feel disoriented and not at all like himself.

"Actually, I'm running a little late this morning," he said. "So we'll have to talk later."

"Stetson!" Adeline swatted his arm. "Where are your manners?" She smiled at Lily. "You'll have to forgive him, Lily. He spends way too much time around uncouth cowboys." She sent him a hard look. "I'm sure he can spare a few minutes for an old friend."

"Fine. A few." He waited for Lily to get to the point, but she shot a quick glance at Adeline.

"Actually, I was hoping we could talk in private."

If Lily wanted to talk in private, she wanted to talk about the kiss. That was the last thing he wanted to talk about. He wanted to forget it. But it didn't look like she was going to let him. He turned on a boot heel and headed to his study, leaving Lily to follow.

As soon as she pulled the door shut, she got straight to the point. "We need to talk about last night."

He leaned against the desk and crossed his arms, trying his damnedest to act nonchalant. "What about it?"

Her gaze fluttered away and her cheeks turned a rosy pink. "I just wanted to make sure you didn't misunderstand what happened. We were having an extremely emotional conversation and I think those emotions just kind of . . . spilled over."

They had more than spilled over. They had combusted. But he didn't say that. Instead, he shrugged. "It was just a kiss, Lily. Nothing more."

Her gaze returned to his. Something flared in her eyes. Something he couldn't quite put his finger on. Anger? Annoyance? Hurt? Whatever it was, it didn't go with her smile.

"Exactly," she said. "It was just a kiss. I wanted to make sure that you didn't think the kiss . . ." She glanced at his mouth. Just the feel of her gaze on his lips had desire settling in the pit of his stomach. He beat it back. "Meant something."

"Nope," he said. "It meant nothing. In fact, most of the night is a little fuzzy. That's what whiskey will do to you."

Her chin came up. "I'm glad we got that cleared up. Last night meant nothing to you and it certainly meant nothing to me."

"Not a damn thing."

Her lips pressed into a flat line, taking all the plump right out of them. He remembered those plump lips. Remembered brushing his lips against them. Remembered licking and pulling them between his teeth. The temperature of his body shot up about twenty degrees. All that heat settled in his crotch. If he didn't get her out of there, the bulge in his jeans would reveal his lies.

"Now if we have that settled," he said. "I have work to do."

Once she was gone, Stetson released his breath and slumped back against the desk. He should be happy they'd gotten that settled. But he didn't feel happy. He felt . . . scared.

The kiss *had* meant something.

More than he would ever admit.

# CHAPTER ELEVEN

*THE POMPOUS ASS!*

Lily had wasted an entire night thinking about Stetson and how she had completely misjudged him. But she hadn't misjudged him at all. He was exactly who she had thought he was: an arrogant beast who enjoyed manipulating people and playing with their feelings.

Not that Lily had any feelings for Stetson.

After a sleepless night, she'd come to the conclusion that the intensity of the kiss had just been a product of their emotional conversation. Stetson had never opened up to her before. His softer side had taken her by complete surprise and screwed with her libido. She wasn't attracted to Stetson. She had never been attracted to him. That was why she had gone over there. She hadn't wanted him to get the wrong idea about the kiss . . . but she also hadn't wanted him to act like the entire night was a mistake brought on by his overindulgence in whiskey. She'd thought they had connected. That they could possibly be friends.

Obviously, she had been wrong.

She flipped a bird at the closed door. "And the little horse you rode in on, Stetson Kingman." She turned around to find Adeline and Gretchen standing in the hallway staring at her. Her face heated. "Sorry. I was just . . ."

Adeline laughed. "No need to apologize. There have been times I've left Stetson's study feeling the same way."

"I can't flip the bird." Gretchen said. "See." She held up her hands to demonstrate. She contorted her fingers in numerous different ways, but none resembled "the bird." She sighed and lowered her arms. "Although it's probably a good thing because my mama would tan my hide if she ever caught me using the F-word—even in sign language." She picked up the bucket with the mop. "Now I better get back to work. You ain't paying me the big bucks to stand around yakking." She headed toward the stairs, the handle of the mop banging the banister as she went.

Adeline watched her with a look of concern before she turned to Lily. "I could use a cup of coffee. What about you?"

A cup of coffee was exactly what Lily needed. Since she'd left her father sitting in the garden doing the morning crossword puzzle, she had the time. "I'd love some," she said and followed Adeline into the kitchen.

While Adeline made coffee, Lily sat down at the island and watched Potts peeling potatoes. The Kingman's cook had been out to the cottage twice since Lily had arrived. Once to bring a plate of his delicious red chile enchiladas and the other to bring a hearty stew. He was a small man with a big beak of a nose and bushy eyebrows. Now that he'd lost his hair on top and the rest had turned gray, he reminded Lily of the Muppet old men who sit in the balcony of the theater and crack jokes. Like the old men, Potts didn't have any trouble giving his opinion.

"I'm glad to see you haven't turned into a complete English tea drinker."

Lily smiled as she watched his nimble fingers manipulate a paring knife around the potato. "I still enjoy coffee, Potts. So do a lot of English people."

He snorted. "They probably sissify it with a lot of cream and sugar like most of the kids do nowadays. Coffee was meant to be drunk black."

Adeline held up the vanilla-flavored creamer she'd just pulled out of the refrigerator where Potts couldn't see. Lily gave a brief nod and changed the subject. "Thanks again for the enchiladas and stew, Potts. Both were amazing."

Potts started cutting up the potatoes he'd peeled. "No problem. I'll bring you and Theo some pot roast and potatoes. That's if the gluttonous Kingmans don't eat it all."

"I'm standing right here, Potts," Adeline said.

"You're the only one not included in that statement, Miss Adeline. You don't eat enough to fill a thimble." He leaned closer to Lily and spoke in a low voice. "She says she's doing just fine, but she ain't." He shook his head. "Not fine at all."

Lily had to agree. Gone was the beautiful, laughing girl Lily remembered. In her place was a pale, sad woman. When they were seated in the sunroom with their coffee, Lily expressed her concern.

"How are you, Adeline?"

"I'm fine."

That's what Lily had told everyone too. But she hadn't been fine. Far from it. She hadn't realized until now exactly how grief-stricken she'd been. She'd thought coming home would increase her pain. Instead, it had started to heal it. Maybe if Lily could get Adeline to talk about her grief it would help.

"If you ever want to talk about Danny, Addie, I'm a good listener."

Adeline smiled sadly. "Thank you, Lily, but I'm really fine. Tell me about England and life as a writer."

Lily spent the next half hour answering Adeline's questions about England and her books. She had just started to tell Adeline about reading to Vivian's class when she glanced out the windows and saw Stetson heading toward the barn and stables. All the annoyance she'd felt earlier came rushing back, and she completely lost her train of thought. The lapse in conversation didn't go unnoticed by Adeline.

"So does your anger at Stetson have something to do with the kiss you and he shared?" Lily choked on the sip of coffee she'd just taken. Adeline leaned over and patted her on the back. "I'm going to assume that's a yes."

Lily stared at her. "Stetson told you?"

Adeline shook her head. "Wolfe. Stetson never

shares anything about his personal life. Not that he has one. You're the first girl he's been interested in for a long time."

Lily picked up a napkin from the tray and blotted her mouth. "Stetson is not interested in me. He's made that perfectly clear." She primly folded the napkin and set it in her lap before picking up her cup again. "And that's fine because I'm not interested in him either."

Adeline studied her for a long moment before she spoke. "Seeing as how you two didn't get along when we were kids, I might believe that . . . if not for Wolfe. My little brother gets a lot of things wrong, but he's kind of an expert on kissing. And from what he saw, he thinks you and Stetson more than like each other."

Lily's cheeks grew warm, and she struggled with how to reply.

"I don't mean to embarrass you, Lily," Adeline said. "But you seemed a little too angry at Stetson this morning to have no feelings for him. And if you're planning on leaving soon to go back to England, then maybe it's best if you and Stetson don't start something that would cause either one of you to get hurt."

Lily hurt Stetson? The idea seemed ludicrous. Her thoughts must've been easy to read because Adeline continued.

"I know Stetson seems like a hard man who can handle anything. But underneath his tough skin is a soft heart. When he cares, he cares deeply. When he gets hurt, he gets hurt deeply."

"I'm not going to hurt Stetson, Addie. You

don't need to worry. There's nothing going on between us. The kiss was a mistake. One that won't be repeated."

Which didn't explain why she was angry with Stetson. She had been so worried he might think the kiss meant something. Why was she now mad that he thought the kiss meant nothing? Obviously, being mad at Stetson was her emotional default. Which was silly. They were both adults. They could share a simple kiss and not make something out of it.

Except there had been nothing simple about the kiss. For the rest of the day, she couldn't shake the memory of Stetson's heated lips on hers.

"What's wrong, Lilliput?" her father asked when she was putting the shepherd's pie she'd made for dinner into the oven. Her father sat at the table with his leg propped up on a chair.

Since she wasn't about to discuss the kiss with her father, she shook her head and smiled. "Nothing is wrong, Daddy."

His eyebrows lifted. "I thought we were going to start being truthful with each other. You're missing England, aren't you? And there's absolutely no reason why you can't go back. I'm doing much better, and Potts and Vivian will keep me well fed."

"I'm not just worried about you being fed. I'm worried about you trying to do too much too soon."

"I'll take it easy."

She took some glasses from the cupboard. "You've never taken it easy. This afternoon proved it. You had no business trying to weed the garden."

"That's the only thing I can do sitting down. I'm tired of not being able to do anything."

"My point exactly."

"I'll be fine, Lilliput. I might be a little slow, but I'm not completely helpless. You need to get back to England and your writing. I've noticed you haven't written at all while you've been here."

She hadn't written. She'd sketched a little, but nothing that had sparked a story. Unfortunately, going back to England wouldn't help. And her father still needed her.

"I'm not leaving," she said. "Not until you're off your crutches. Now how about if we eat in the garden tonight?"

Lily hadn't eaten in the garden since her mother had passed away. Gwen had loved eating breakfast, lunch, and dinner in the garden when the weather permitted. The three of them would sit around the patio table and talk and laugh long after the food was gone. It was time Lily and her father continued the tradition.

She turned on the outside lights and lit a candle for the table, then opened a bottle of Merlot to go with their shepherd's pie. It was her mother's recipe. The comfort food and wine seemed to relax Lily and her father and they talked more than they had ever talked. When they finished eating, her father leaned back in his chair and glanced around the garden. The full moon hung high in the sky and the lights strung in the trees gave the garden a magical feel.

"Your mother loved this place, didn't she?" he said. "After she passed, it was so hard to work here. Gwendolyn was everywhere. In every flower that bloomed and every leaf that fell." He smiled sadly. "But now I realize that she's not in the garden." He touched his chest. "She's here. And she always will be. Even after I marry Vivian."

Lily reached out and took his hand. "I love you, Daddy."

He smiled at her. "I love you, too, Lilliput."

They finished off the wine, enjoying each other's company and the moonlit spring night. Then her father helped her stack the dishes and she carried them inside while he held the door and shut off the garden lights.

In the kitchen, her father stopped at her mother's china cabinet. "You should probably pack all your mom's teacups and teapots while you're here. I'll have them shipped to you. Along with anything else of your mother's that you want."

She started to fill the dishwasher. "I guess Vivian will want to bring her own things when she moves in."

Her father cleared his throat. "Actually, Lilliput, I'm thinking about moving in with her."

Lily stopped loading and looked at him. "What? But who will take care of the garden?"

"I'm sure the Kingmans won't have any trouble finding another gardener." He smiled weakly. "I never was a gardener, Lilliput. That was your mother."

"That's not true, Daddy. Look how beautiful the garden is."

He looked out the window. "All I do is water it and do a little pruning, mulching, and fertilizing. Your mother was the genius behind the beauty. She loved plants and flowers."

"What are you going to do?"

"Vivian said the janitor at the school is retiring at the end of this year. I think I'll apply for the job. I like being around kids."

Lily didn't know what to say. She had always thought her father loved gardening as much as her mother had. Now he was telling her that he didn't. And he was leaving the cottage just when Lily had realized how much she loved the little stone house and all the memories it held. This was her home. This would always be her home. She couldn't stand the thought of someone else moving in and changing the little English kitchen or getting rid of the fairy garden.

As if reading her thoughts, he sighed. "I know you love this house. I love it too. It will be hard to leave it. But you have your life in England, and I'm ready to let the past go and move on."

As hard as it was to accept, she knew he was right. "You should move on. We both should." She hugged him and held tight for a long moment before she drew back. "Now you need to go to bed. You've done way too much today."

"My leg is starting to ache a little." He gave her a pat on the arm. "It will be okay, Lilliput. I'm sure Stetson will let us visit the garden anytime we want to."

Lily knew he would too, but it wouldn't be the same.

After her father left, she finished putting the dishes in the dishwasher and then stepped out into the garden. How could her father leave this? But she knew the answer before she even finished thinking the question. He was leaving because it was time to start a new life with Vivian.

As much as she understood that, it was hard to let go.

Leaving the lights out, she moved down the steps and walked along the dark path, breathing in all the familiar scents of flowers and lush vegetation. The temperature had dropped since she and her father had eaten dinner. A cool breeze rustled the leaves overhead. She glanced up at the branches of a solid oak tree. The same tree she had climbed to peek into Wolfe's bedroom window, hoping for a glimpse of her teenage crush. She smiled at the memory, but her smile faded when she saw the shadowy form amid the branches.

There was someone in the tree.

"Stetson?"

But it wasn't Stetson who jumped to the ground in front of her. This man was shorter and stockier. He wore a cowboy hat pulled low on his forehead, which wasn't unusual for a ranch. What was unusual was the bandana he had covering the lower part of his face.

Fear hit Lily the exact second the man's hands closed around her throat and he shoved her back against the trunk of the tree.

She tried to fight, but he pinned her efforts beneath the weight of his body and growled close to her ear. "I don't want to hurt you. You aren't one of them."

But even as he said the words, his hands tightened on her neck. If she didn't do something, she knew she would end up dead. She lifted her foot and brought her heel down as hard as she could on the instep of his foot. His hands loosened their hold and he stepped back far enough for her to jab a knee into his groin. If she hadn't been so focused on escape, she might've enjoyed his grunt of pain. As soon as he let her go, she took off down the path. She wasn't about to lead the man to her father so she headed in the opposite direction of the cottage.

To the one person she trusted to save her.

# CHAPTER TWELVE

SINCE STETSON HADN'T SLEPT MUCH the night before, he should've been exhausted. But after Wolfe, Buck, and Delaney left to play poker in the bunkhouse and Adeline went upstairs to take a long bath after a hectic day of trying to train the new housekeeper, Stetson felt restless, not tired. He thought about reading by the fire in the great room. Reading always calmed him. But as soon as he stepped into the room, he was assaulted with images of Lily and their explosive kiss. Needing to walk off some of his energy, he grabbed his hat and headed out the back door. He had only gotten a few steps toward the stables when he heard Lily scream his name.

"Stetson!"

The fear in her voice told him something was wrong way before she appeared out of the darkness and flung herself into his arms. Her entire body trembled like a leaf in a strong wind.

He held her close. "What happened? Is it your father?"

She shook her head against his chest and spoke in a gasping voice. "A m-m-man . . . attacked me

. . . in the g–g–garden."

Stetson didn't know if he had ever felt the rush of anger he'd felt at that moment. It was like a red–hot wave of fury that started in his gut and spread through his entire body. But he couldn't release his anger now when Lily was so frightened.

He held her tighter and tried to absorb some of her fear. "I got you, Lily. No one is going to hurt you now."

The back door opened and Adeline stepped out in a bathrobe. "What's going on?"

"Lily was attacked in the garden."

"Oh my God! Is she okay?"

Before Stetson could answer, Gage came running up. "I heard someone screaming."

Before Stetson could answer, Adeline snapped at Gage. "It was Lily. Someone attacked her in the garden. I thought you were keeping an eye on the ranch. Isn't that what we pay you for?"

Gage drew back. "Yes, ma'am. It is what you pay me for." He looked at Stetson. "I'll check out the garden." He turned and ran off.

Stetson wanted to go with him in a bad way, but he couldn't leave Lily. Not when she was still trembling. He looked at Adeline. "Call Wolfe and have him round up the ranch hands to help Gage."

"We need to call the sheriff, Stetson."

"I know. I'll do it as soon as I take care of Lily."

Adeline placed a hand on his arm. "Maybe I should take care of Lily."

It made sense. Lily probably would be more

comfortable telling his sister what happened. But Stetson couldn't seem to bring himself to let her go. And she didn't act like she wanted him to. She clung to him, her arms tightly clasped around his waist and her cheek pressed to his heart.

"I got her." He started to pick her up and carry her into the house, but Lily stopped him and drew back.

"My father. I need to make sure my father is okay."

"Gage will check on him."

Lily shook her head. "He'll be worried about me if Gage shows up without me."

Stetson took her hand. "Okay. I'll go with you." As they drew closer and closer to the garden, Lily's fingers clenched tighter and tighter on his. Rather than lead her through the place where she'd been attacked, he took her around to the front. Once inside, they found Theo fast asleep in his bed.

"He must've taken one of his pain pills," she whispered as she tucked the sheet around him. "There's no need to wake him."

Stetson didn't agree. But he waited until they were in the kitchen before he voiced his opinion. "I think your father will be upset if you don't wake him up and let him know what—"

Lily turned to him and Stetson cut off as he got his first real look at her. Her hair was mussed and her face pale as death. But it was the angry red welts encircling her neck that really blew the lid off his anger.

"I'm going to kill the sonofabitch," he growled.

He might've charged out to the garden to see if he could get his wish if Lily hadn't reached out and taken his arm.

"I'm okay, Stetson."

"You're not okay. The asshole tried to kill you." His gaze ran over her body. "Where else did he hurt you?" He returned to her eyes. "Did he rape you, Lily?"

"No. He just choked me." She touched her neck and winched in pain.

Concern overrode his anger, and he pulled out a chair from the table. "Sit down and I'll get you some ice."

He went to the refrigerator and got a bag of frozen corn from the freezer. When he returned, she was sitting in the chair staring out the kitchen nook window at the garden. He crouched in front of her and gently placed the bag on her neck.

"You okay?"

She gave him a wobbly smile. "Just a little sore."

He let her take over holding the bag of corn and pulled out a chair to sit down. He hated to have her relive what she'd been through, but if they were going to find the person who'd done this, they needed all the details. "Can you tell me what happened? Did you recognize the man?"

"I couldn't see his face. He wore a black cowboy hat pulled low so it shadowed his eyes and a red bandana over the lower part of his face."

Most of the cowboys on the ranch had black hats and red bandanas. Stetson and his brothers included.

"Was he a big man? Small?"

"He was stocky and muscular."

"He just jumped out at you?"

"No. I was walking in the garden and I glanced up and saw someone in the branches of the old oak. At first, I thought it was you."

"Me? What would I be doing hiding in a tree?"

She shrugged. "Spying? I used to spy on your family all the time from that tree."

"You mean you used to spy on Wolfe all the time." A smile lifted the corners of her mouth. He was glad to see it. He couldn't help teasing her. "Why you little Peeping Lily."

She laughed, and some of the tension in his shoulders eased. "What can I say? I was a hormonal teenager with a major crush." She lowered the bag of corn, but he lifted it back to her neck.

"It will help with the swelling." He tightened his fingers around hers and gently squeezed. "I'm sorry, Lily."

"It wasn't your fault, Stetson."

"I should've seen it coming after what happened with Tab."

"Tab? What happened to Tab?"

He released her hand. "Someone broke into the stables and when Tab came to see what was going on, whoever it was hit him over the head and knocked him out. We think it was the same person who started the barn fire and killed our bull, Bobby Tom."

Lily stared at him. "Someone killed a bull and purposely set the barn on fire?"

"Theo didn't tell you?"

"No. I saw the ranch hands working on the

barn, but I thought you were just replacing the roof. Daddy should've told me."

"I'm sure your father didn't want you to worry about him when you headed back to England. Which is the same reason I didn't tell him about Tab. I thought with his busted leg, he had enough to worry about. But if I had warned you and Theo, tonight wouldn't have happened."

She lifted her hand and rested it on his cheek. It was cold from the bag of corn, but it still started his heart thumping madly. "You aren't responsible for keeping the entire world safe, Stet."

It was the first time she'd used his nickname. He liked the way it sounded coming from her lips. His gaze lowered to those lips, and the memory of the kiss they'd shared flared to life—bringing with it a strong desire for a repeat. But just as Stetson leaned in, light flooded in through the window. The garden was crawling with ranch hands. If they hadn't found the culprit by now, he was long gone—as would be any evidence the man left behind once it was trampled beneath so many boots.

What had the man been doing in the tree? Had he been lying in wait for Lily? Or had he been lying in wait for someone else and she'd just caught him? Either way, the man had crossed a line. Stetson wasn't going to give him the opportunity to hurt anyone else.

He got to his feet. "Until we catch the guy, you and Theo are going to stay in the guestrooms at the house. Go pack some things for you and your dad. I'll go wake up Theo."

"I'm not leaving the cottage, Stetson."

"Yes you are."

Lily stood and got that stubborn look on her face that Stetson was starting to recognize. "No I'm not. I get that you like to tell everyone what to do. But you're not my boss. I'm staying at the cottage. Especially since it might be the last time I get to stay here."

"What do you mean?"

A sad look entered her eyes. "My father plans to move in with Vivian once they're married."

Stetson was shocked. Theo hadn't mentioned a word about leaving the ranch. "But he can't leave. He's family. I'll talk to him about it. The ranch is his home."

Lily placed a hand on his arm. "Thank you, Stetson. Thank you for giving him a home for all these years. I know he thinks of you as family too. But as much as I love the cottage and will miss coming back here, I don't want you to talk him out of leaving. The night I arrived, you called me selfish. And I have been. I was so worried about my own grief that I didn't take into consideration my father's. He's been through so much and he deserves to be happy and have a fresh start with Vivian without being surrounded by memories of my mom."

Stetson agreed Theo deserved a fresh start, but he hated that it had to be away from the ranch. He had always counted on Theo being here for him. Theo leaving just didn't feel right. Lily never coming back to the cottage again didn't feel right either. But he couldn't deal with it tonight. There were other things he had to deal with.

"Fine," he said. "I'll stay here."

Lily's eyes widened. "What?"

"If you insist on staying in the cottage, then someone needs to keep an eye on you and your father."

"You don't have to do that, Stetson. Now that I know men are hiding in the trees waiting to jump out at me, I'll be more careful. And I proved tonight that I can take care of myself. Whoever choked me will have some bruised private areas tomorrow."

Stetson stared at her. "You kicked him in the balls?"

"Kneed him. That's how I got away."

He laughed. He'd never taken Lily for a fighter. Of course, she loved to fight him at every turn. But he couldn't let her fight him on this.

"I'm staying, Lily. I'm going to see if Gage and the boys have found anything, and then I'll be right back." He headed for the door before she could argue. As soon as he stepped into the garden, Buck and Wolfe came to greet him.

"How's Lily?" Buck asked. "Did that bastard hurt her?"

Stetson nodded. "She has his handprints around her neck."

Wolfe growled. "When we find him, I want him first."

"After me, little brother. And after I get ahold of him, there won't be anything left." Stetson looked around. "Did you find anything?"

Buck shook his head. "Gage said he found a few

boot prints in one of the flowerbeds, but those could be anyone's. So why was the guy after Lily? She doesn't have anything to do with the ranch."

"I'm not sure he was after her. I think she just caught him." Stetson paused. "I think he was after one of us."

"I wished he'd caught me," Wolfe said.

Stetson turned to his brother. "If he sneaks up behind you like he did with Tab, you might not fare any better. Which means we need to be careful. And we need to keep a close eye on Delaney and Adeline. I'm not too worried about Addie. She stays close to home. But Delaney runs around like a wild mustang. That's going to stop."

Buck snorted. "Good luck with getting her to listen. She's as stubborn as the day is long and does whatever she pleases. You shouldn't let her play poker in the bunkhouse, Stet. It's no place for our sister."

Wolfe laughed. "You're just mad because she took all your money."

"She took everyone's money! She had all of Jasper's chips in the first hour. Mine in the second. And that just ain't right to take money from family."

"Aww, poor Buck." Wolfe patted him on the shoulder. "Should I call the wa-a-ambulance?"

Buck shoved Wolfe away. "Shut up."

"Both of you shut up," Stetson said. "This no time for arguing. I don't care how stubborn Delaney is. Where she goes, you go, Buck." He looked at Wolfe. "And the same with you and Addie."

Wolfe's eyes narrowed. "If we're stuck babysitting our sisters, what are you going to be doing, Stet?"

"I'm going to stay here at the cottage and watch out for Theo and Lily."

Wolfe smirked. "And what happened to you staying away from Lily?"

"After tonight, I don't have a choice."

"Yeah, you do. I could stay at the cottage."

"Leave it alone, Wolfe," Stetson warned.

"Wait a second," Buck said. "Why would you want to stay away from Lily? You called first dibs on her, Stet. If you've decided you don't want her, I'm calling second dibs. I'll stay at the cottage."

Before Stetson could tell Buck there were no dibs, Wolfe slung an arm around Buck's shoulders. "I'd be careful, little brother. Stetson doesn't like people laying claim to his woman."

"She's not my woman," Stetson said.

Wolfe grinned. "You just keep telling yourself that, big bro." He tightened his arm around Buck's neck and gave him a noogie on top of the head. "Come on, pipsqueak, let's go check on our sisters."

When they were gone, Stetson went and found Gage. Adeline's words had done a number on him. He looked guilty as hell.

"I'm sorry, Boss. Your sister's right. I fell down on the job. I got . . . distracted and wasn't paying attention."

Stetson placed a hand on his shoulder. "Adeline didn't mean it, Gage. She was just upset about Lily. You aren't responsible for what happened. With the trees in the way, there's no way you could've seen what was going on in the garden. Even from your perch on the scaffolding. If anyone is to blame, it's me. I assumed that whoever it is wasn't brazen enough to harm people. After what happened to Tab, I should've known better." He pulled out his cell phone. "Whether I want to or not, it's time to call the sheriff."

As usual, Sheriff Dobbs was little help.

"It sounds like you boys did all you can do for the time being." Sheriff Dobbs yawned loudly. "Me and Tater will come by first thing in the morning and take a look around. I've got a keen eye for finding things most folks can't. Although you sure this wasn't just a drunk cowboy looking for a little slap and tickle? Lily Daltry was always a foreigner. You know how loose some of those European gals can be."

Stetson gritted his teeth. "Are you saying she asked to be attacked?"

"Now don't go getting your feathers ruffled. Just making a point. I'll see you in the morning."

Once the sheriff hung up, Stetson rammed his phone back in his pocket and cussed under his breath all the way to the cottage. When he got there, Lily wasn't in the kitchen. He figured she'd gone to bed. He locked the door and turned out the kitchen light. He left the lights on in the garden.

In the living room, he found a pillow and comforter on the couch. After using the hall bathroom, he stripped down to his boxers and socks and tried to get comfortable. His feet hung off the end and the cushions were too soft. Still, it had been a long day and, with the little sleep he'd gotten the night before, he nodded off quickly.

He woke what felt like only minutes later. He glanced around trying to figure out where he was and what had woken him. Then he heard it. A soft moan. He quickly got up and headed down the hallway to Lily's room. He found her tossing and turning, obviously in the midst of a nightmare. Probably the same nightmare she'd just lived through.

He hesitated for only a moment before he crossed the room and climbed into bed. She had held him when he needed holding. He figured he could return the favor. As soon as he pulled her into his arms, she quieted and burrowed against his chest. The bed was as short as the couch. His feet hung off the end and his head butted the wood headboard. And yet, Stetson had never felt so comfortable.

He pulled her closer and buried his nose in her soft hair. "I got you, Lily."

# CHAPTER THIRTEEN

LILY WOKE TO THE AROMAS of cooking bacon and brewing coffee. Since her father didn't drink coffee, she wondered if she was still dreaming. She'd had a wonderful dream the night before. A dream of being nestled against Stetson's hard, naked chest and listening to the cadence of his breathing and the thump of his heartbeat as he soothingly stroked his fingers through her hair.

She buried her face into her pillow and sighed with contentment. A scent filled her nose. A scent she recognized immediately. Her eyes flew open and she sat up. Pain shot through her neck, but she barely registered it as she stared down at the white pillowcase with the single short brown hair resting on it.

Stetson *had* been in her bed last night. He *had* held her close and soothingly stroked her hair. He *had* whispered sweet comforting things.

She smiled.

The beast wasn't a beast. And maybe he never had been. Maybe he'd just been a boy grieving for his mother and angry over his father's betrayal and unable to deal with either emotion.

"Mornin'."

Her gaze shot to the doorway where Stetson stood. There was no sign of the beast this morning. With the sun reflecting off the copper streaks in his hair and the whiskey flecks in his eyes, he looked every inch a prince. A prince who had held her when she'd needed holding.

Suddenly, she remembered exactly how his body had felt pressed against hers. Like a solid wall of hard, toned muscle covered in a light dusting of dark hair. His chest hair hadn't felt coarse against her cheek as much as satiny. When she'd shifted in his arms to get more comfortable, it had tickled her nose . . . along with the scent of virile man. She had never known what virile man smelled like until Stetson. It was a mixture of fresh air, horses, and rich earth.

Did he smell like that today? She suddenly had the urge to press her nose to the spot where his western shirt lay open.

"Lily?"

She pulled her gaze from the tan skin of his throat to find him staring at her with a concerned look.

"Are you okay?" he asked. "You look a little flushed. Maybe I should take you to see a doctor."

Lily blinked and tried to clear the lusty thoughts from her head. "No, I'm fine. I always wake up a little . . . hot."

His gaze lowered to her mouth, but then quickly returned to her eyes. "I made you some breakfast if you want it."

"You cook?"

"Only on rare occasions. Which explains why the bacon is overcooked and the scrambled eggs under. The coffee is good. Since your father doesn't have a coffeemaker, I had Potts bring it down from the big house."

"I would love a cup of coffee. And I happen to like my bacon extra crispy and my eggs slightly underdone."

"That's exactly what your father said." He flashed a smile, and her stomach did a crazy little flip-flop.

She tried to focus. "My father's up? Did you tell him what happened?"

"I had to explain why I was sleeping on his couch."

"And how did he take it?"

"Like any father would. He was concerned, and then ticked off that we didn't wake him last night. He came to check on you earlier, but you were still asleep. He's outside talking to the sheriff right now."

"Did the sheriff find anything?"

He snorted. "No, and I'm not surprised. The man's as inept as his deputy." His gaze lowered to her neck. "But we'll find who did it. I promise you that. Now come eat before your eggs get any worse tasting than they already are."

The eggs weren't as bad as Stetson made them out to be. In fact, they were delicious. Or maybe they just tasted delicious because Lily was so hungry. Stetson didn't join her for breakfast. Once he set her coffee and plate down on the table, his cell phone rang and he excused himself and moved to the living room to take the call.

She had just gotten up to pour herself some more coffee from the thermos that sat on the kitchen island when her father came in the back door. She expected him to give her a lecture about not waking him up last night. Instead, he balanced on his crutches and pulled her into his chest with one arm.

"I'm so sorry, Lilliput."

She nestled closer. "It's okay, Daddy. I'm fine." He drew back and looked at her neck. His features tightened with anger and she tried to calm him. "It looks worse than it feels."

Her father studied her neck for a few seconds more before he glanced over her shoulder. "Find him, Stetson."

Stetson walked into the kitchen. "I plan to, sir."

Thankfully, that was the end of the discussion on what happened the night before. While Lily finished eating, her father and Stetson sat at the table and talked about the new foal and spring branding. Lily was surprised her father knew so much about both. She was also surprised Stetson seemed to value her father's opinion. Several times during the conversation, he asked what her father thought. His deep respect for Theo was obvious. When her father brought up leaving the ranch and moving in with Vivian, Stetson quickly tried to talk him out of it.

"You can't leave, Theo. I can't run this ranch without you."

Her father smiled. "Don't blow smoke up my

butt. You've been running this ranch just fine without any help from me. Or anyone else." He put a hand on Stetson's shoulder. "You're a damn fine rancher, son."

Stetson's cheeks turned a bright pink. It was the first time Lily had ever seen him blush. Once again, her heart did a crazy little somersault. "Thank you, Theo," he said. "But I still have a lot to learn."

"Don't we all, son." Theo patted his shoulder. "Anytime you want to talk things over, you'll know where to find me."

Stetson sighed. "So I guess there's no talking you out of moving?"

Her father smiled. "No, but I'm glad you like me enough to try." He glanced at Lily. "Although I'm thinking someone might've put a bug in your ear."

"As much as I'll miss the cottage, I understand why you want to move in with Vivian after you get married," Lily said. "Have you thought about a date?"

Her father got a funny look. "Actually, we have."

"When?"

He swallowed. "How does this next weekend sound?"

As much as she had accepted her father getting remarried, it was still a little painful to have it happening so fast. "This next weekend?"

"We thought we'd do it while you're here. That way, you won't have to interrupt your writing to come back for a wedding. And I want you here for the wedding, Lilliput. I won't do it without your blessing."

She pushed any remaining reservations she had away and leaned over to give him a peck on the cheek. "You have my blessing, Daddy. I think this weekend will be perfect."

His relief was obvious. "I thought we could have it here in the garden. Of course, now that's probably not a good idea. The garden no longer has good memories for you."

He had a good point. Even looking out the window at the oak tree made her feel a little queasy. But she refused to let some jerk ruin her love of the garden. Or her father's wedding day.

"I'm fine, Daddy. I think a garden wedding is a great idea."

Unfortunately, Stetson didn't. "I'm sorry, but I don't think it's a good idea to have the wedding at the ranch when there's still some madman running around wanting vengeance."

"But surely he wouldn't try something when people are around," she said.

"I can't chance it."

"Stetson's right," her father said. "We'll have the wedding in Vivian's backyard and invite fewer people." He looked at Stetson. "I was wondering if you'd be my best man."

Stetson looked taken back. "Me? Are you sure?"

Her father laughed. "You're the best man I know."

"Then it would be an honor."

Her father got up. "I guess I better go call Vivian and tell her to start planning."

When he was gone, Stetson turned to Lily.

"Are you okay with your father getting married so quickly? I know it's hard to think about him loving someone besides your mother."

"It is hard, but I know Vivian will make him happy. After so many years of being alone, he deserves some happiness."

Stetson's eyes grew intent. "And are you happy in England, Lily?"

It was a good question. She had thought she'd been happy writing away in her in little Surrey cottage. But in the last couple weeks, she'd come to realize how empty her life had been in England without family and friends. Or a man who made her feel breathless and needy.

Before she had to answer, Stetson's cell phone rang. He got up from the table and answered it. When he was finished with the brief call, he slipped his phone back into this pocket and turned to her.

"I need to head to the stables. I'd like you to stay here and keep the doors locked, but since you are about as good at listening to what I say as my sisters, you'll have to come along."

Just the thought of going to the stables had Lily almost dropping the plate and coffee mug she'd just picked up. She knew her fear of horses was silly, but she couldn't seem to help it. "You don't need to babysit me, Stetson. I'm going to write in the garden today." Or try to.

Stetson released an aggravated huff as he followed her to the sink. "Why am I surrounded by stubborn women? Delaney called this morning to tell me there was no way in hell she was going to put up with Buck babysitting her. An hour later, I got the same phone call from Adeline about Wolfe. Now, I'm all for women's rights. But when it comes to the safety of the women in my family, I have to draw the line. Buck and Wolfe are sticking to my sisters like glue and I'm sticking to you, Lily. You want to write outside, you can write in the stables where I can keep an eye on you. I'm not going to make you ride a horse. You can sit in one of the empty stalls and work."

*Surrounded by huge, unpredictable horses. No, thank you.*

"I'll lock the doors and stay inside with my father," she said as she turned on the water and started rinsing her plate.

"Please don't tell me you're scared of even being around horses." When she didn't answer, he turned off the water and pulled her around to face him. His dark eyes didn't hold humor or ridicule. They held understanding . . . and determination.

"You're right. It doesn't make sense that you grew up on a horse ranch and are scared of horses. Don't you think we should remedy that? There's this cute little fella I think you should meet."

Lily didn't know how Stetson talked her into it—maybe because he refused to take no for an answer—but an hour later, she was watching him lead a little horse out of the stables. The foal still looked big to Lily, and she took a few steps back as they approached.

"This here is Majestic Glory's son," Stetson said

with pride in his voice. "Twenty-seventh son to be exact."

"Twenty-seventh?" Lily eyeballed the horse, whose head barely came up to her shoulders. "That's a lot of siblings."

"That's not even counting his sisters." Stetson patted the foal's withers. "You have a big family, don't you, boy?"

The foal bobbed his head as if in agreement, then turned curious brown eyes on Lily. He was pretty cute. She took a step closer. "What's his name?"

"His new owners get to name him. We just call him Glory Boy." Stetson held out his hand. "Come here, Lily. He won't bite."

There was a time when Lily wouldn't have trusted him enough to take his hand. But now she didn't hesitate. He pulled her closer to the horse. As if sensing her nervousness, the foal danced away a few steps and Lily drew back. But Stetson held the lead rope as securely as he held Lily's hand. When both horse and woman had settled, he guided Lily between him and the horse and placed her hand on the foal's soft, warm back.

"See." Stetson's breath fell softly against her ear he moved her hand along the horse's back. "There's not a thing to be scared of."

Her heart continued to thump rapidly beneath her ribcage, but that wasn't due to the horse's nearness as much as Stetson's. And mixed with her desire was a warm feeling of security. She realized she trusted him. She'd trusted him to save her last night. And she trusted him to make sure this baby horse wouldn't eat her today.

"I'm still not going into the stables," she said.

His deep chuckle vibrated against her back.

"Then I guess we'll just have to spend our day outside with Glory Boy."

"I thought you had work to do."

"I do. But it can wait. It's too beautiful a day to waste inside." He released her hand, but didn't step away. He continued to stand close as if he wanted to be there in case she needed him.

Lily had once thought she'd never need Stetson Kingman for anything.

But now she wasn't so sure.

# CHAPTER FOURTEEN

"JUST SHOOT ME NOW AND put me out of my misery." Wolfe flopped down in a chair at the cottage kitchen table Stetson had set up as his office and covered his face with his hands.

Stetson sighed and closed his laptop. "Stop whining, Wolfe. It's only been three days."

"Three days of hell."

Stetson ignored his brother's complaining and glanced out the window to make sure Lily was still lying in the hammock sketching. He grinned when he saw she'd fallen asleep with her sketch-pad resting on her chest and her pencil dangling from her fingers.

Wolfe lowered his hands. "Are you listening, Stet?"

He returned his attention to Wolfe. "I don't believe you're in hell. If you had to keep an eye on Delaney, that would be one thing. But Adeline doesn't give anyone any trouble."

Wolfe stared at him. "It's not our sister who is driving me crazy. It's the new housekeeper."

"Gretchen? What did she do?"

"What doesn't she do is more the question.

She's constantly sneaking around the house and popping up where you least expect her. She walked right in when I was showering the other day."

"It's not like a million women haven't seen you naked, Wolfe," Stetson said dryly. "I'm sure Gretchen was mortified."

"That's just it. She didn't act mortified. She acted like it was all part of her job." Wolfe spoke in a high-pitched voice with a thick southern accent. "'Excuse me, Mr. Kingman, but I forgot to put fresh towels in here and I certainly wouldn't want you to catch your death runnin' around as nek-ked as the day you was born.'" Wolfe's eyes widened in horror. "She then proceeded to stand there holding out the towel like she expected me to step out of the shower and let her dry me off like a toddler straight out of the bath."

The image made Stetson laugh. "Obviously, she's taking her job seriously. We can't fault her for that."

"Yes I can. She's creeping me out, Stet. I don't feel comfortable in my own house. I want you to fire her. I asked Adeline to do it, but she flat refuses."

"I'm not going to fire someone for trying to do the best job they can, Wolfe. If you don't want her walking in on you, lock the door."

"I swear I did lock the door!"

"That's ridiculous. She didn't pick the lock just to see you naked."

Wolfe ran a hand through his hair. "I'm not so sure about that. She acts all sweet Southern innocence, but something is not right with that woman."

"Maybe you're just upset because she hasn't fallen under your charm."

Wolfe snorted. "The last thing I want to do is charm Gretchen Flaherty. I'm telling you she scares the hell out of me." Stetson couldn't help it. He burst out laughing. Which made Wolfe scowl. "Go ahead and laugh. I'm stuck in hell while you get to stay out here at the cottage and play house with Lily."

That sobered him. He glanced back out the window. "We're not playing house."

"I don't know what else you'd call it. I've seen you two wandering around the garden at night like an old married couple." Wolfe's eyebrows waggled. "Or Adam and Eve before the fall."

"We're just talking."

It wasn't a lie. He had talked more to Lily in the last few days than he had talked to anyone in his life. They talked about everything. About their childhoods, high school, college, and their lives after college. Surprisingly, their lives had been very similar. They both spent the majority of their time focused on work. They hadn't partied. Or gotten sucked into the world of online dat–ing. Or even off-line dated. But at least Stetson had his family and the people he worked with to keep him company. It sounded like Lily had no one.

The thought of her going back to her lonely life bothered him more than he was willing to admit. She didn't belong in England. She belonged on the ranch. Of course, once her father married, she would no longer come to the ranch. That bothered him as much as her going back to England did.

"If I had Lily in a dark garden, you better believe I wouldn't be talking." Wolfe's words pulled Stetson back to the conversation.

"Get your mind out of the gutter," he warned.

But he had no business getting after Wolfe when there were times when Stetson's thoughts about Lily were anything but pure. Late at night, when he was lying on the uncomfortable couch just a few feet from where Lily slept, his mind took a trip straight down the gutter, fantasizing about doing all kinds of naughty things. Sometimes, it didn't even wait for night. Sometimes, it conjured up those fantasies during the day.

Like right now, when he imagined what it would be like to walk out into the garden and kiss Lily awake. Would she push him away or pull him down into the hammock with her?

The back door flew open, and Stetson cringed when he saw Delaney stomp in with Buck right behind her.

"I'm telling you, Stetson," his sister bellowed. "If you don't keep Buck away from me, I'm going to strangle him to death."

"Not if I strangle you first, you madwoman." Buck held the door for Adeline. Stetson was surprised to see his oldest sister . . . and happy that she'd finally made it out of the house. Even if it was only to the garden cottage.

"Both of you lower your voices," Adeline said.

"This isn't our home."

"It will be when Theo leaves." Buck's arm shot up like a kindergartener wanting to be picked first. "I call first dibs!"

"You don't get the cottage, dickhead," Wolfe said. "Whoever we hire as the new gardener gets it."

"Why can't the new gardener live in the bunkhouse? I want my own space." He glared at Delaney. "I'm tired of sharing space with a nutcase."

"If you don't like it, then leave." Delaney waved a hand. "And good riddance."

Stetson sighed and rubbed his temples. He loved his family, but sometimes they were hard to take. "No one is leaving. The new gardener will get the cottage." Even though the thought of some stranger living here didn't sit well with Stetson either. "And if the only reason y'all are here is to complain, then you can all leave. I have work to do."

"I'm not here to complain," Adeline said. "I just found out that Theo and Vivian's wedding is going to be in Vivian's small backyard. I think it's appalling that you didn't offer the garden for the wedding, Stetson. This is Theo's garden as much as it's ours. He's the one who's tended it all these years. The one who keeps it so beautiful for us to enjoy. This is where he should get married. Surrounded by all his friends and family."

Stetson agreed, but he couldn't risk someone getting hurt. "Theo understands the circumstances, Addie."

Adeline crossed her arms. "I don't give a damn about the circumstances. What's right is right."

"Ooh," Delaney chimed in. "Adeline cussed. You're in trouble now, Stet."

Adeline shot Delaney an annoyed look before she turned back to Stetson. "The wedding is going to be here in the garden. I've already called Vivian to let her know. If you need to get with your henchman and have him set up better security during the wedding and reception, that's up to you. But the wedding will be right here." She turned and walked out.

Dead silence reigned after the door slammed shut.

Then Wolfe spoke. "It looks like Addie is coming out of her depression."

A few days later, the garden was teeming with people all dressed up in their Sunday best.

Stetson stood in Theo's bedroom looking out the window. He should be worried about the man who wanted vengeance on the ranch doing something during the wedding. Instead, his mind was on something else entirely.

Lily was leaving in less than two days.

She'd told him the night before as they were cleaning up the dinner dishes. He had continued to place the rinsed plates she'd handed him into the dishwasher as if a thick band of depression hadn't tightened around his heart. As if her leaving wasn't a big deal.

But it was a big deal. Much bigger than he ever

could've imagined.

"You look more like a groom about to give up his single life than I do, Stetson."

Stetson turned to Theo and pinned on a smile. "And you don't look anything like a nervous groom."

Theo crutched his way closer. "I thought I would be, but all I feel is . . . happy. And a little guilty for feeling so happy."

Stetson moved away from the window. "Guilty? Why?"

"There's a part of me that feels like I'm cheating on Gwen." Theo shook his head. "I know it's crazy. But when you've been happily married to someone, it's hard to move on. Even when they're long gone."

Stetson had never understood how Theo's marriage could be so happy when his wife had been having an affair with another man. But this wasn't the day to think about the past. He put his grievances against Gwen aside and gave Theo his full support.

"You have nothing to feel guilty about, Theo. You loved Gwen and were a good husband to her." He paused and told a little white lie. "And she loved you. When you love someone, you want them to be happy. If there is an afterlife, I figure she's up there in heaven wishing you the best."

Theo smiled. "Thank you, Stetson. And thank you for keeping such a close eye on Lily the last few days. Especially since I'm not quite in fighting condition." He glanced down at the cast on his leg.

"No problem. I've enjoyed staying at the cottage. It's been a nice reprieve from my arguing siblings."

Theo laughed. "I can only imagine." He hesitated. "And speaking of arguing, it seems like you and Lily are getting along much better than you did when she first got here."

They were. With the way Stetson felt, he wasn't sure that was a good thing. Maybe it would've been better if he'd kept his distance. Maybe then he wouldn't be feeling like a gutted fish at the thought of her leaving. When he didn't say anything, Theo continued.

"I haven't heard Lily laugh so much since her mother passed. And how did you get her to go into the stables?"

"Glory Boy is responsible for that. He wiggled his way right into her heart. Then all I had to do was talk about how cute he was with his mama and what a shame it was that Lily couldn't see them together."

Theo laughed. "Good for you. It was time she got over her fear."

Lily wasn't completely over her fear. She still refused to get close to the adult horses. If Stetson had more time, he knew he could get Lily riding. But he didn't have more time. His time with Lily had almost run out.

It was all he could think about during the wedding ceremony. Lily looked stunning in her soft green maid of honor dress. He couldn't take his eyes off her—even when she glanced over and caught him staring. He wanted to memorize every one of her perfect features. After Theo and Vivian were declared man and wife, he could think of only one thing: being with Lily.

But the guests converged on the bride and groom to congratulate them, and Stetson lost sight of her. Then Adeline showed up in a panic because the bartender she'd hired hadn't shown up.

For the next couple hours, Stetson was stuck tending bar . . . and watching Lily as she played hostess and walked from group to group visiting with the guests. She'd always seemed so shy as a kid. But now he realized she wasn't shy. She just didn't ramble on like some folks. She talked when she had something to say. When she didn't, she was okay just listening. She was a great listener. Which probably explained why Stetson had talked to her more than he had talked to anyone else.

He wanted to talk to her now. And more than that, he wanted to hold her. And he wanted her to hold him. He wanted to get in all the holding before she had to leave and he never got to hold her or be held by her again.

"Well, you Kingmans sure know how to throw a weddin'."

Stetson pulled his gaze away from Lily to find Kitty Carson standing at the table set up as the bar. She wore a bright green striped dress. Coupled with her red hair, she looked a little like a Christmas Who from Whoville. "Hello, Miss Kitty." Stetson said. "Can I get you something to drink?"

She held up her glass of punch. "No thanks. I'm not much of a drinker after my daddy died of liver disease." She shook her head. "A cryin' shame. Just a cryin' shame. So have you heard about Jim Davis? Squirrels got in his rafters and peed and pooped so much that it rotted out the ceiling. Entire thing caved right in while he and Elma and their six kids was eatin' Sunday supper. Totally ruined Elma's mac and cheese. Of course, her mac and cheese never has been as good as she thinks." She shook her head and tssked. "Such a cryin' shame. And then there's what happened to poor Dean Whitley. Bless his heart. He got the worst case of warts you ever did—"

Jasper walked up before Kitty could finish her story and Stetson had never been so happy to see his cousin. "Hey, Stet. Don't tell me you're going into the bartending business. If so, I'd be happy to trade places with you. I'll ranch and you can bartend for my grumpy grandfather."

Stetson laughed. "With my bartending skills, I'd put Nasty Jack's out of business in a week. In fact, would you mind taking over for me? There's something important I need to do."

Jasper shook his head. "I fell right into that one." He moved around the table to change places with Stetson.

"Thanks, man. I owe you."

"You sure do," Jasper said. "And one day, I'll collect."

"Just don't make the payment too steep." He looked at Kitty. "Sorry to run off, Miss Kitty. You let me know if I can do anything to help Jim and

Dean."

Stetson headed straight over to where he'd last seen Lily. But she was no longer chatting with Vivian's brother's family. Nor was she talking with any of the other guests. He started to grow concerned. What if the man who had attacked her was one of the guests? What if he *had* been after Lily all along and had lured her away?

His heart beat overtime as he continued to search the crowd. He was just about to gather a search party when he walked past the steps that led down to the hedge labyrinth and saw her maid of honor bouquet and a half-empty glass of champagne sitting on the stone ledge.

He hurried down the steps and into the maze.

Having played there as a kid, he knew his way through it. He knew the shortest route to the other side and where the break in the hedge was that led to the very center of the maze. He wasn't surprised to find Lily there. All the King-man women loved the small secret garden with its mosaic-tiled fountain. Lily was sitting on the edge of the fountain, trailing her fingers through the water. In the gauzy pastel green dress with her hair pinned up in loose curls and the sun-set sky washing her perfect features in shades of orange and gold, she looked like one of her mag-ical fairies.

Not wanting to startle her, he spoke softly. "Did you know that fountain came all the way from the Middle East? It's rumored to have belonged to a sheik with fifty wives."

Lily turned to him and smiled. "That story has

to be something you and your brothers thought up."

He laughed and moved closer. "Wolfe to be exact. He's always dreamed of having fifty wives." He sat down next to her. "Or maybe not wives— just women."

"I'd say he's probably reached his goal and then some." She looked down at her fingers trailing in the water. "My mother told me a different story about the fountain. According to her, it had once belonged to fairies who lived in an enchanted forest."

"Is that where your fairy stories came from? Your mother?"

She nodded and continued to trail her fingers in the water. "I used to throw every penny I found into this fountain. Fairies love glittery things. Especially shiny coins. The fairies hoard all the coins, but once a year, they choose one coin and grant that wish."

Stetson smiled as he looked down at the layer of coins beneath the water. "So you're the one who got my sisters to throw the change from their piggy banks into the fountain."

Her gaze lifted to his. "I seem to remember seeing you toss a penny or two."

He shrugged. "I've always been one to hedge my bets."

"Did the fairies grant your wishes?"

He shook his head. "No. They didn't give me superpowers . . . or keep my mother from dying."

Her eyes filled with tears. He hated that he could make her cry so easily. "I didn't get that wish either." She hesitated. "But I did get one of my wishes."

"And that was?"

She smiled a quivery smile that tore at his heart. "You don't hate me anymore."

No, Stetson didn't hate her. What he felt for Lily was as far from hate as you could get. The realization scared the hell out of him. Especially when she was leaving. If he were smart, he'd say something clever and take her back to the reception.

But he wasn't smart.

Not where Lily was concerned.

He slid his fingers into the silky strands of hair that had fallen around her face and drew her closer. When their lips were a breath away, he whispered,

"You got your wish, Lily."

# CHAPTER FIFTEEN

WHEN LILY HAD TOSSED THE penny into the fountain and made her wish, she'd never dreamed the fairies would grant it close to eighteen years later. And so completely. There was not a trace of the hateful boy she'd grown up with in the kiss Stetson gave her. It was soft and tender and made her feel like the most cherished woman in the world.

Lily was lost. Lost in the sweet sips of his lips. And the gentle pressure of his hand on her waist. And the soft caress of his fingers in her hair. There was no hungry rush or greedy need. There was just this slow, languid mating of mouths.

And yet, it was even more erotic than the passionate kiss they'd shared in front of the fire. That kiss had been solely fueled by physical desire. This kiss was fueled by something else. Something that left Lily breathless and trembling like the last leaf of autumn trying to hold on. She was scared of what would happen if she let go and completely gave herself over to Stetson. But she was more scared of leaving and never knowing where these intense feelings would lead.

She moved her hand from where it rested on his knee and cradled his jaw, loving the way his rough stubble felt against her palm. He was rough, but as everyone had tried to tell her, beneath all the roughness was a tender heart that Stetson hid well. As the oldest, he felt like he had to be the strongest. The most mature. The one who kept all his true emotions inside. He'd hidden his father's betrayal. He'd hidden his fear of running a huge ranch. He'd hidden his loneliness. But he didn't have to hide from her.

The fact he was showing her such tenderness proved it.

Her heart swelled with emotion and she had the strong desire to put those feelings into words. Instead, she drew back just enough to whisper against his lips.

"Stetson." There was so much power in that one word. As a kid, it had struck fear in her heart. As a teenager, it had consumed her with annoyance. Now . . . and forever, it would hold all the overwhelming feelings of this moment.

She didn't know how long their lips continued the slow, erotic dance. She was only vaguely aware of the sun's warmth disappearing and the night's cool arriving. Of the soft trickle of the fountain and the gentle brush of a breeze. Even when their secret place was discovered, she was so focused on Stetson she barely registered the intrusion.

"Umm . . . sorry, Boss. I hate to interrupt, but everyone is pretty worried about you and Lily."

Stetson continued to kiss her for a moment

more before he drew away. She opened her eyes to find him looking at her with such longing she felt lightheaded.

"Thanks, Gage," he said without looking away from her. "We'll be right there."

"Yes, sir."

"And Gage. I'm counting on your discretion."

"Didn't see a thing, Boss."

Once Gage was gone, Stetson brushed a strand of hair from her cheek and studied her lips. "I guess we need to get back."

"I guess we should."

His gaze lifted. "Maybe later, we could pick up where we left off . . . I mean if you want to."

He was giving her the choice. She could leave the garden and never kiss him again. Or she could meet him later and do this all over. She knew what the smarter choice was. She was leaving. Starting something up with Stetson was pointless. But with her lips tingling and her heart pounding, it didn't feel pointless.

It felt right.

She looked into his eyes, eyes that reflected the moon that had risen without her even being aware. "I want to."

The smile he gave her took the rest of her breath away. She continued to feel breathless as he took her hand and led her back through the dark maze. When they reached the end, he gave her one more thorough, leisurely kiss before he whispered against her lips.

"Later."

Most of the guests had left by the time Stetson

and Lily got to the garden. Just the Kingmans, Gage, her father, and Vivian remained—and a few cowboys who were helping take down the tables. Lily felt instantly contrite when she saw how relieved her father was when he saw them.

"You two had us worried sick, Lilliput," he said. "Next time you and Stetson want to wander off, you need to let someone know."

Wolfe grinned. "Yeah, Stet, you shouldn't just sneak off without a word."

While Lily's face burned with embarrassment, Stetson spoke with his usual calm. "Lily and I went to check on Glory Boy. On the way back, Lily bet me that she could get through the maze faster. Y'all know I never can turn down a challenge."

"Nope," Wolfe said with a sparkle in his eye. "You never can turn down a challenge, big bro"

Something passed between the brothers before Adeline spoke. "Well, we're glad you're safe." She looked at Theo and Vivian. "Now you two can get to your honeymooning."

"Actually, I think it might be best if Vivian and I stayed at the cottage tonight." He glanced at Stetson. "My leg is feeling much better and think I can handle an intruder if need be. I'm sure you're ready to sleep in a comfortable bed instead of on a hard sofa."

Stetson shot a glance at Lily. She knew exactly what he was thinking. The cottage would've been a perfect place to continue what they'd started. Now, her father had thrown a wretch in their plan. Like he knew exactly what had been going on in the maze and wasn't about to let it continue.

"The sofa isn't so bad," Stetson said. "And I hate for you and Vivian to change your plans of staying at her house tonight."

"It's no problem," Vivian placed an arm around Theo's waist. "I know Theo wants to spend as much time as he can with Lily before she leaves."

Stetson smiled weakly. "Of course he does."

Lily was just as unhappy about the turn of events. As everyone helped with clean up, her gaze continually wandered over to where Stetson and his brothers were taking down tables and folding chairs. He had removed his suit jacket and rolled up the sleeves of his light blue dress shirt. She couldn't see his eyes in the shadow of his black cowboy hat, but she knew when he discovered her watching him. He froze in the middle of folding a chair and she felt the heat of his gaze even from twenty feet away. Her lips tingled and she sucked in her bottom lips hoping to taste some remnant of Stetson's kisses.

The chair slipped from his fingers and clattered to the ground as he started toward her. As he drew closer, she saw the determined look in his eyes. She knew he was going to kiss her right there in front of everyone.

And she was going to let him.

But before he could reach her, Vivian walked up. "Do you have a minute, Lily?"

Lily looked at Stetson, who had come to a dead stop only feet away with a hungry, needy look in his eyes. She felt just as hungry and needy, but she couldn't say no. Stetson must've realized this because he turned on a boot heel and strode off while she looked back at Vivian.

"Sure. What did you need?"

"I just wanted to say thank you." Vivian's eyes dampened with tears. "I know today wasn't easy for you, and yet, you couldn't have been a sweeter maid of honor or a more gracious hostess to all our family and friends. God didn't bless me with children of my own, but I feel like He has blessed me with one now."

Lily's heart squeezed, and she gave Vivian a tight hug. "Thank you. I feel just as blessed to have the teacher I already loved as my stepmother."

"Stepmother." Vivian laughed as she drew back. "That sounds kind of ominous, doesn't it? I'll try not to make you do the dishes and mop the floors too often when you come for a visit."

Lily laughed. "You're too nice to be a wicked stepmom."

"You haven't seen me when your father forgets to put down the toilet seat." Vivian glanced around, and her eyes turned sad. "I know he's going to miss this place and all the memories he made with you and your mom. I told him I'd be happy to move here, but he insisted on moving in with me until we can look for a house of our own."

As much as Lily would've loved them living in the cottage, she knew it wasn't the best thing for her father. "He's right. You two need to make your own memories."

Vivian sent her a sly look. "Speaking of making

memories. Just what were you doing with Stetson Kingman in that maze, young lady?"

Before she had to answer, her father walked over. "What are my two favorite girls whispering about?"

"None of your beeswax, Mr. Daltry." Vivian gave him a quick kiss on the cheek before she winked at Lily. "Girls are allowed to have their secrets."

When the cleanup was finished, all the Kingmans left together—including Stetson. Obviously, he'd given up on continuing where he and Lily had left off. She couldn't blame him. Every time they had started toward each other someone else had interrupted. It was almost like fate was sending them a message.

A message Lily paid absolutely no attention to.

Once Vivian and her father were in bed, Lily went to her room and lifted the sash and slipped out the window. She still wore her dress, but she left her shoes behind. She didn't want the heels clicking on the tile stairs and alerting the entire house.

But she never made it to the house. Halfway up the pathway, she spotted a man moving toward her. She might have been scared if she hadn't recognized the broad shoulders and determined stride. He halted for a moment when he saw her, then his steps quickened. He lifted her into his strong arms as his lips covered hers.

"Damn," he whispered against her lips. "I couldn't wait a second more for this."

"Me either." She bit his bottom lip and tugged

it between her teeth.

He groaned and his hands gripped her butt cheeks and lifted her completely off her feet. The hard bulge Lily felt in his jeans made her faint with desire. She pressed against the lengthy ridge.

"Jesus," Stetson breathed. He talked between lush kisses. "I hope . . . I'm not . . . being . . . presumptuous . . . but I . . . really want . . . really want . . . to take you . . . to my bed."

Lily brushed her tongue against his. "I insist."

He chuckled. "What a control freak you are, Lily Daltry."

He carried her inside and up the long staircase without stopping their kissing for more than a few seconds to open the back door. Once they were in his room, he didn't let her go. He closed the door with his foot and then pushed her back against it.

"I want you so damn bad." He kissed his way down her neck, the scruff of his beard sending a shiver of heat through her. "So damn bad." He kissed the spot behind her ear before sucking it into his mouth. The shiver of heat spread like a wildfire and pooled between her legs. She wrapped her legs around his waist and pulled him even closer, rubbing against his rigid hardness. The friction of his denim against the damp spot of her panties had the fire quickly escalating until it exploded into a shower of sparks.

She cried out and Stetson captured the cry with his mouth. Only after she released her legs and wilted against him, did he pull back from the kiss. She was more than a little embarrassed by how quickly she had reached climax and her cheeks flamed.

"Sorry," she said. "I haven't had a lot of experience with . . . this." In fact, she'd only had sex a few times. Once at Oxford with a fumbling college student who hadn't even given her an orgasm. And a couple of times with the café waiter who had been more experienced, but had never made her feel the way Stetson did.

His eyes softened, and he gave her a gentle kiss. "Then we'll take it slow." He sent her a sexy smile before he lowered to his knees. His hands skated up her thighs lifting her dress as they went.

"Stetson, I don't think I can—" She cut off when the warmth of his breath infiltrated the damp crotch of her panties. A second later, his mouth settled on the spot and desire ricocheted through her. He tongued her through the silk and she arched away from the door and closer to his mouth.

"You don't think you can what?" His words were muffled.

She gasped as his tongued flicked again. "Nev-er mind."

He continued to tease her to madness through the thin veil of her panties before he slipped them down her legs. Then there was nothing between her and his hot, wet mouth. He hooked one of her legs over his shoulder, leaving her open to whatever he planned. He planned to drive her wild with intimate kisses as slow and intense as the ones he'd given her mouth. He took his time sipping at her center until her leg trembled and her body jerked with need. Then he focused his attention on the quivering bud at the top. With just a few strokes of his tongue, she rocketed into another orgasm.

When it was over, her legs gave out. He scooped her up in his arms, carrying her to the biggest bed she'd ever seen in her life.

As if reading her thoughts, he laughed. "I know. It's huge. My granddaddy liked big things." He set her on the fluffy down comforter. Then proceeded to strip off his clothes. When he was completely naked, Lily had to agree with King Kingman.

Big things were nice.

Stetson was big. And perfect. She had never seen such a perfect man. She wanted to sketch every detail from the top of his tousled dark hair to the broad toes of his long feet.

Her thoughts became words.

"I want to sketch you," she said.

"I think you already have."

She stared at him. "You looked in my sketchpad."

"Guilty. And I believe you took some creative license. I don't have that many muscles, honey."

She got up. "Well, let's see." Taking her time, she ran her hands along his shoulders and down to his biceps. She enjoyed their hard flex before she slid her hands back up to his shoulders and traced along his collarbone before gliding down to cradle each pectoral muscle.

His eyes had closed, and she could hear his heavy breathing as she teased his nipples with her thumbs. Then she slid her hands down along the two columns of his ripped abs. Her own breathing escalated.

"I'm thinking you have plenty of muscles, Stetson Kingman." She took his hard length in hand. "Plenty."

His breath grew even more ragged as she caressed his erection from base to tip. "You're killin' me, baby," he groaned.

"Good." She fisted him tightly and stroked. She had just found a rhythm when his hand covered hers.

He kissed her deeply and whispered against her lips. "I want to be in you." He drew back from the kiss and lifted her dress over her head, leaving her in nothing but her lacy bra. With only a twist of his fingers, it joined her dress on the floor. His breath came out in a rush. "Damn, you're beautiful."

"So are you."

He laughed. "You're sex-drugged, Lily. I'm far from beautiful."

"No, I'm not." She cradled his face, her thumb caressing his scarred cheek. "I didn't see you before. But I see you now. I see your beauty."

His smile faded. "Sweet Lily. You make me believe it." He leaned in and kissed her. The kiss was as gentle as the ones in the maze. But this time, his hands freely wandered over her naked body, caressing her skin like he was trying to memorize every inch. When he had her wet and wanting, he drew her down to the bed.

His lovemaking was as tender as his kisses. He

didn't pound or quickly pump. Instead, he moved his hips in smooth undulations that left her feeling like she was floating in a sea of hot desire. It was only after she'd reached her pinnacle that he quickened his pace and followed with a deep groan and a hard shutter of release.

He rested against her, his lips pressing into the spot where her neck met her shoulder for a brief second before he pushed up to his hands. He was smiling. Not the usual tip of lips, but a wide, toothy grin that crinkled the corners of his eyes and showed off one dimple in his scarred cheek. With his hair falling over his forehead, he looked younger than he'd ever looked. Young and adorable.

She reached up and smoothed a strand of hair back. "And just what are you grinning about, Stetson Kingman?"

"If I had known how good you were in bed eight years ago, I wouldn't have let you leave."

# CHAPTER SIXTEEN

STETSON WOKE TO A FEELING of excitement. The kind of excitement he'd felt as a kid when he'd woken up on Christmas morning knowing that soon he'd be unwrapping his presents. He opened his eyes and looked at the best present he'd ever received.

Lily was a bed hog.

She slept on her back with her arms and legs sprawled out at all angles. One hand rested on the pillow above her head while the other was draped over his neck. Her left foot hung off the bed while her right foot hooked over his ankle. Her mouth was slightly open and a little rumble of a snore huffed out on each exhale, fluttering the ebony strand of hair that fell across her lips.

Stetson pushed up to his elbow and smoothed the strand away. It slid through his fingers like silk, reminding him of the night before when he'd fisted the strands in his hands as she'd taken him into her mouth and sent him flying. His grandfather had always said that still waters run deep. It was true in Lily's case. She had turned out to be anything but Shy Lily in bed. He might have to start calling her Wild Lily.

He glanced at the clock sitting on the night-stand. He should probably wake her so she could sneak back into her room before her father dis-covered she was missing . . . and so Stetson could get to the mile-long list of things that needed to be done today on the ranch. But Lily looked so comfortable he couldn't bring himself to wake her. Or maybe it was his comfort he was more concerned with.

He didn't want her to leave. He didn't want her to leave now. And he especially didn't want her to leave on a plane tomorrow. She didn't belong in England. She belonged right here. With him. He didn't know what that meant. All he knew was it was the truth.

She fidgeted in her sleep, her foot shifting on his leg and her hand prodding his chest. Her eyes fluttered open. She stared at the ceiling for a few seconds before a contented smile slid over her lips. A smile that made his heart quicken. It almost beat right through his ribcage when she turned her head and her sleepy gaze met his.

"Good morning."

There had never been more accurate words spoken.

He smiled. "It is. A very good morning."

A blush painted her cheeks a cotton candy pink he wanted to taste. "What time is it?"

"Early." Too early for her to leave. He slid his hand over one soft breast and cradled it in his palm, brushing her nipple with his thumb. Her green eyes were no longer sleepy. The spark of heat in them melted any thought of letting her go.

He shifted and pulled her into arms, but she covered her mouth before he could kiss her.

"Morning breath."

He laughed. "Then I'll just have to think of someplace else to kiss you."

He found a lot of places to kiss. The soft skin of her neck. The sweet curves of her breasts. The stiff peak of each nipple. The cute indention of her belly button. And the wet, warm heat between her legs.

When her hands fisted the sheets and breathy little "ahhs" escaped her lips, he switched from kissing with his lips to kissing with his tongue. Watching her hit her climax was one of most beautiful things he'd ever seen. And the hottest. He waited for her to melt into the mattress before he sat up to get a condom from the nightstand. He was surprised when she leaned over his shoulder and took it from him.

Once it was on, she shoved him back on the bed and straddled him. Lily might be afraid to ride horses, but she wasn't the slightest bit afraid to ride him. She rode him hard. She rode him until he was completely broke and willing to go wherever she led. She led him to a mind-blowing orgasm that had him moaning out her name. When every last hot spark had fizzled to a contented tingle, she covered him like a blanket and held him tight.

He could've stayed wrapped in her arms forever.

Pressing his face into her hair, he breathed her in. She smelled like the garden—vibrant and alive. If she left, he could never walk through it without thinking about her and this moment. Which meant he would have to go back to avoiding the garden. He didn't think he could live with that.

"I probably need to get back to the cottage," she said.

His arms tightened, and he said what he felt. "Don't go back to England, Lily."

She lifted her head and blinked. "What?"

He plunged on, babbling more than he had in his life. "Stay here—at least a little while longer. You can stay at the cottage. I don't even have to sleep with you if you don't want . . . I'll sleep on the couch. I'm just not ready for you to leave yet. And you said that you're having trouble writing anyway. And considering your books are set on a ranch, it makes much more sense for you to be inspired here than inspired in the English countryside. Maybe you just need to get out and see the ranch to get inspiration for another story. I would be happy to show you around all the places that fairies might like to play. But we just need a little more time . . . just a little more time."

Her hesitation made a lump form in his throat. It dissolved quickly when a smile spread over her face. "Okay."

He stared at her. "Okay?"

She nodded. "I'll stay a few more days."

A few more days didn't sound like nearly enough time. But he'd take what he could get. He kissed her. A thank you kiss for the night. And the extra days. And for being Lily. But just as it was getting steamy, she drew away.

"I really need to go, Stetson. I don't want my dad to see I'm gone and worry."

As much as he wanted to stay in bed with her all day, he knew she was right. "I'll walk you to the cottage."

He hoped he'd get the pleasure of watching her clothe her petite, sexy body, but she disappeared into the bathroom and he was left to dress alone. When she came out, she walked straight over to him and gave him a long, deep kiss that tasted like fresh mint.

He drew back and smiled. "Did you use my toothbrush, Lily Daltry?"

She looked appalled. "Of course not. I just used your toothpaste."

He pulled her closer. "You can use my tooth-brush anytime, sweetheart. I like sharing germs with you." He gave her another kiss before he took her hand and led her to the door. Once he'd made sure the coast was clear, he drew her out into the hallway.

"This feels familiar." He teased her as they silently moved down the hall.

She giggled, and then quickly covered her mouth. "It does, doesn't it? But you weren't nearly as nice the last time you snuck me out of this house."

"Maybe I was just mad it wasn't me you showed up naked for."

Lily shot him a startled glance just as Adeline stepped out from her room. She froze when she saw them. Stetson figured there was no lying about Lily just stopping by to say hi when she was barefoot and wearing a wrinkled maid of honor dress. So he held tight to her hand and went with it.

"Mornin', Addie."

His sister stared at him and then at Lily, whose face had turned a bright tomato red. Thankfully, Adeline wasn't the type to make a scene or cause anyone undue embarrassment. She pinned on a smile. "Good morning. Potts is making his famous blueberry pancakes this morning." She looked at Lily. "I hope you'll stay for breakfast."

Lily cleared her throat and tried to get Stetson to let go of her hand, but he wasn't letting go. "Thank you. But I really need to get back to the cottage."

"Of course. Now if you'll excuse me, I forgot something." She stepped back into her room and closed the door.

"That was so embarrassing," Lily said when they were heading down the hallway again.

"Adeline won't say anything if that's what you're worried about."

"It's not just that. No woman wants to be caught sneaking out of a man's room."

Stetson thought about her words all the way to the cottage. They didn't sit well. When they spotted Theo in the garden and Lily jerked Stetson around the side of the cottage so they wouldn't be seen, he really got annoyed.

"Are you ashamed of liking me, Lily?" he asked when they were standing by her bedroom window.

She looked surprised by the question. "Of course not. I just think it would complicate things if everyone knew."

He lifted his eyebrows. "Why? We're both adults. If we want to spend time together, that's nobody's business but ours." He cupped her chin and brushed his thumb over her lips. "And I want to spend time with you, Lily. Do you want to spend time with me?"

Her answer came on a warm breath that caressed his thumb. "Yes."

The Christmas morning feeling came back, and he smiled. "Okay then." He leaned down and kissed her. It was hard to break away from her sweet lips, but finally he did. Once he helped her back in the window, he kissed her again before he took his leave. He got exactly three steps away from the cottage when he started missing her. Suddenly, all the things he needed to get done that day weren't all that important.

He walked around to the garden and found Theo sitting on a bench sipping a cup of tea. His friend usually had a smile for him. Today, he didn't. Instead he had a hard look that said he'd peeked into Lily's room and discovered her missing. Since she had been with Stetson when she'd gone missing the night before, it probably hadn't taken much to put two and two together.

Stetson felt his face heat. He took off his cowboy hat and cleared his throat. "Lily was with me last night."

"I figured as much. And I want to know your

intentions, Stetson. Lily is an adult, but she's still innocent. I won't have you taking advantage of that innocence."

"It's not like that, Theo. I like Lily. I like her a lot. I should've come to you sooner and told you that I wanted to date her, but I've never been good at understanding my own feelings." He shook his head. "Hell, I'm still not good at it. All I know is that I want to spend more time with your daughter."

"And how do you plan to do that when she's leaving?"

"I talked her into staying longer."

Theo studied him for a moment before he nodded. "Okay. But you hurt her and I'll kick your ass up one side and down the other. Broken leg or not."

"I wouldn't expect otherwise."

There was a long, nerve-wracking stretch of silence before Theo picked up his teacup. "So what's going on with that stud you were thinking about buying?"

Stetson's shoulders relaxed, and he joined Theo on the bench. They fell into a comfortable conversation about the stud until Vivian stepped out the back door of the cottage.

"So this is where you disappeared to." She gave Theo a soft smile before she greeted Stetson. "Good morning, Stetson. I found some instant coffee for us folks that need a bigger caffeine kick than tea. Would you like a cup?"

"I would love one," Stetson said. "Straight black is good." When she was gone, he turned to see

Theo still looking at the door with a dopey sparkle in his eyes.

It was easy to see he loved Vivian. But he'd also loved Gwen. Which proved you could fall in love with more than one person in your lifetime. Maybe that's what had happened to his father. Maybe Lily was right. Maybe his dad had said all the hateful things to his mom in anger and hadn't meant any of them. He'd just never gotten a chance to take them back.

Stetson knew what that felt like. At his father's funeral, there were things Stetson wanted to take back. Douglas hadn't been the best of fathers, but he'd been the only one Stetson had. Something Stetson hadn't realized until he was gone.

The back door opened again, but this time, it wasn't Vivian who stepped out. This time, it was Lily. She had showered and changed into snug jeans and a pretty pink shirt that matched the blush on her cheeks when she saw him.

"What are you doing here?" she asked.

"I decided to take the day off."

She looked confused. "But Stetson Kingman doesn't take days off."

He smiled. "He does now."

# Chapter Seventeen

"WHAT PART OF 'I AM not getting on a horse.' don't you understand?"

Stetson led the beautiful—but scarily huge—chestnut horse a few steps closer to Lily. "I'm not asking you to ride it by yourself, sweetheart. I'm asking you to ride with me." His eyes twinkled beneath the brim of his cowboy hat. "Your fairies ride dragonflies. That has to be much scarier than riding a horse. Especially Beetlebub's dragonfly. That wild thing tosses him off all the time."

Her eyes widened. "How do you know that? Have you read my books?"

He shrugged. "Your dad gave me the first one and I sorta got hooked. I couldn't wait to see what horrible thing Beetlebub was going to do to Poppy." He cocked an eyebrow. "Beetlebub? Did that happen to come from Beelzebub? Which is another name for the devil? Was I really as mean as the devil to you, Lily?"

Heat flooded her face. "You know."

"The scars he got on his cheek from running into a rosebush were kind of a dead giveaway."

Her blush grew brighter. "I'm so sorry, Stetson. I didn't really know you when I wrote those books."

He held up a hand. "It's okay, Lily. I deserved it. I was pretty hard on you. But I want you know it had nothing to do with you. It was just displaced anger I had for . . . someone else."

"Who?"

He shook his head. "It's not important."

Now Lily was intrigued. He'd told her about being angry with his father, so it had to be someone else. Who else had Stetson been angry with? And why had he taken that anger out on Lily? Before she could ask, he pulled her into his arms for a thorough kiss that left her mindless. When he drew back, there was something in his eyes that made her feel even more loopy.

"All that matters is that Beetlebub and Poppy have figured out they like each other," he said. "I like you, Lily Daltry. I like you a lot."

Her breath locked in her chest. "I like you too, Stetson Kingman. A lot. And if it's any consolation, Beetlebub is one of my most popular characters. Every Halloween, I receive hundreds of pictures of kids dressed up in cowboy hats and black wings." She smiled. "I guess everyone likes a naughty boy."

He laughed. "Me naughty? It wasn't me who got naughty last night. You won't ride a horse, and yet, you rode me like a champion bronc rider."

She glanced around the stable yard to see if anyone was listening. The only people around were Tab, who was working with a horse in the paddock, and Jasper, who was standing on the fence watching. She swatted Stetson's arm. "Would you hush up? Someone might hear you."

"I don't care if they do."

He didn't seem to care. He flaunted their relationship to everyone. Including his family. Last night, he'd invited her to dinner at the castle and made it perfectly clear to everyone that they were a couple by not letting go of her hand when they walked in, constantly leaning over to whisper sweet nothings in her ear during dinner, and pulling her onto his lap once they moved to the family room to play games. His siblings spent the entire evening staring at him as if he'd grown horns.

She understood why. Gone was the man who put work before play and rarely smiled. In his place was this man who spent the last few days entertaining her with afternoon picnics, leisurely drives in the country, and late night stargazing. A man who smiled a lot and laughed even more.

A man who had charmed his way right into Lily's heart.

It felt like much more than like. The feeling was scary, and at the same time, wonderful. Especially when he looked at her like he was looking at her now. Like she was special.

"Do you trust me, Lily?"

She nodded, and he gave her one more kiss before he lifted her up into the saddle. Before she could panic about being on such a big beast, he swung up behind her and tucked his arm securely around her waist.

"I'm right here, honey. I'm not going to let you

go." With a flex of his thigh muscles, he nudged the horse into a walk. As he walked the horse around the yard, Lily hung onto the saddle horn for dear life. She held on even tighter when he steered the large animal out of the yard into an open meadow. He leaned over and whispered in her ear. "We're not going any faster, sweetheart. Rooster doesn't like to run. He likes to take his time and enjoy the view." He lifted his arm and pointed. "See the hawk?"

She glanced up to see a hawk, with its wings spread wide, floating in the clear blue Texas sky. As they went, Stetson continued to point things out to her. An armadillo scuttling across the road. A bright colored lizard sunning itself on a rock. A cactus with flowers as frilly as a child's pink tutu.

Awed by the beauty around her, Lily forgot about her fear. She'd been so busy hiding away in the garden she'd missed God's bigger garden. She now understood why her father had argued with her mother about Lily spending too much time at the cottage. She had missed out on so much. All because she was afraid to take a step outside her comfort zone. Her mother had thought she was helping her introverted daughter by keeping her close and entertaining her with fairy stories. But that had only made Lily live in her fantasies rather than in this beautiful reality.

When they got back to the stables and Stetson helped her off the horse, she placed her arms around his neck and kissed him, infusing the kiss with all the emotions that tumbled around inside her. Stetson drew back and his eyes held enough heat to melt the sun.

"Let me get Rooster unsaddled," he said in a low sexy voice, "and I'll meet you at the cottage."

Lily couldn't think of anything better than spending the rest of the afternoon in Stetson's arms. When she got to the cottage, she let herself in through the back door. An open box sat on the island, surrounded by teacups and pots. While she waited for Stetson, she packed the ones she wanted to ship to England.

England.

It had once seemed like the perfect haven. A place where she could get over her mother's death. But now she realized that England hadn't been a haven as much as a hiding place. Just like the garden had been. And hiding from her grief hadn't helped her get through it. It had only prolonged it. It wasn't until she came home that she'd started to heal.

Now she was leaving again.

Why?

She knew she had a book to finish, but what made her think she could finish it in England when she hadn't been able to write one word before she'd left? Maybe Stetson was right. Her fairy books were set on a prairie, not in the English countryside. If anything was going to inspire her writing, it was the landscape she'd just traveled through today. Even now, her mind whirled with a storyline about Poppy making friends with a lost armadillo and getting a majestic hawk and a lazy lizard to help her find Arnie the Armadillo's home.

She stared at the teapot she'd just started to wrap in bubble wrap. Was she actually thinking about staying in Texas?

It was crazy, but that's exactly what she was thinking. Her family was here. Her father and Vivian were both getting older. If something happened to them, she needed to be the one who took care of them. She *wanted* to be the one to take care of them.

And then there was Stetson.

She didn't know where their relationship was going, but she wanted to find out. They certainly couldn't do that through long distance phone calls. They needed time together. She wanted to give them that time. She couldn't ask to live in the cottage. And she wasn't about to live with her father and Vivian when they were newlyweds. But maybe she could find someone in Cursed who would be willing to rent her a room. At least for a few months. Kitty Carson would no doubt know of someone.

Suddenly, she felt like a heavy weight had been lifted off her shoulders. Instead of finishing wrapping the teapot, she decided to make tea to celebrate her decision. But when she took off the lid to place teabags in the pretty china pot, she discovered it was filled with folded notes. She took one out and read it.

*Sweetheart, Meet me in the maze at midnight.*

Lily smiled. Her father might not be a talker, but it looked like he could write love notes. But the next note she read confused her.

*Sweetheart, I miss you every second of every day.*

*And I hate that we can't be together.*

Why would her father write that? He and Gwen had lived and worked together? A bad feeling settled in her stomach. The feeling grew as she read the next note.

*Sweetheart, we can't confess to Theo and Elizabeth. Think of what it would do to our children.*

Lily stared at the note with her heart in her throat. Her mother had been having an affair. And the name Elizabeth told her exactly who her mother had been having an affair with. A memory flashed into her mind. A memory of Stetson standing in front of a fire telling her about the argument his parents had had the night his mother died. Everything made sense now.

"Lily?"

She glanced up to see Stetson standing just inside the door. She had been so tangled in the sticky web of her discovery she hadn't heard him come in. Lily had the strong urge to stuff all the notes back in the teapot and pretend she had never seen them. But it was too late. Like Pandora's Box, Gwen's teapot had already been opened.

All the vile things couldn't be shoved back inside.

"It was my mother," she said in a voice that held all the pain and disbelief swirling around inside her. Her hand shook as she held up the note. "My mom was the one your father was having an affair with." When Stetson didn't act surprised, she had her answer. Tears burned the back of her eyes, but she refused to let them fall. "Why didn't you tell me?"

"Telling you wouldn't have changed anything, Lily."

"It would've explained why you hated me."

He went to reach for her, but she stepped away. His hand dropped back to his side. "I was wrong. You weren't to blame. If anyone was to blame, it was my grandfather for forcing my father into a marriage with a woman he didn't love." He stepped closer. "But it doesn't matter, Lily. It doesn't matter because it's all in the past. What happened between our parents shouldn't affect us."

Stetson was right. It was in the past and it shouldn't matter. Especially when her father was now married to Vivian. But it did matter. It mattered to Lily. The perfect mother she thought she had hadn't been perfect at all. She'd had an affair with another man. If she had kept all his notes, she had loved Douglas. And how could she not? Lily knew firsthand how hard it was to resist a Kingman.

She could picture her prim-and-proper mother arriving from England with her quiet, somber husband and shy, introverted daughter and being swept off her feet by the charming, charismatic cowboy prince of Kingman Castle.

It looked like history had repeated itself.

Stetson had swept Lily off her feet and had her falling head over heels for a man who could never truly love her back. How could he when her mother was responsible for his mother being on that icy road? And maybe a long-term relationship with her had never been part of his plan.

He liked her, but he never said anything about love. Probably because he knew a serious relationship with her would be ill-fated from the start. If she had known about their parents she never would've let herself fall for Stetson. Because regardless of what he said, the past never stayed in the past. Once the fresh blush of sexual attraction wore off, Lily would just be the daughter of the woman who had destroyed Stetson's family.

With tears clogging her throat, she turned and headed to her bedroom where she pulled a suitcase from the closet.

Stetson moved into the doorway. "What are you doing?"

"What does it look like I'm doing? I'm packing." Luckily, she didn't have much to pack. She felt like all the air was being squeezed from her lungs and she needed to get away from Stetson and Kingman Ranch so she could breathe again.

"You're going back to England?"

"That's where I live." She finished tossing in her clothes. But before she could zip up her suitcase, Stetson took her arm and stopped her.

"I get you're upset, but we need to talk about this if we're going to fix it."

She jerked away from him. "Talk about it? So now you want to talk about it? We should've talked about it long before now. If I'd known about my mom and your father, I never would've gone to bed with you."

He flinched as if she'd slapped him. "What they did has nothing to do with us."

The tears she'd been trying so hard to hold

back welled into her eyes. "What they did has everything to do with us. Their affair affected your entire life . . . which affected mine. You can't deny that."

He pulled off his cowboy hat and ran a hand through his hair. "Okay, I admit that it screwed me up. But I've figured things out now."

"Have you? What have you figure out, Stetson?"

"I've figured out that you're nothing like your mother. You're sweet and kind and good."

A tear rolled down her cheek. "My mother was sweet, kind, and good." And she'd had an affair with another man. Lily just couldn't fit that piece of the puzzle into the mother she knew.

"I need to go." She zipped her suitcase and pulled if off the bed, but Stetson refused to move out of her way.

"I can't let you leave, Lily. You're in shock— believe me, I know. And I don't think it's a good idea for you to travel right now, sweetheart."

If he hadn't used the same word his father had used in the notes, the thin thread Lily was holding onto might not have snapped. But it did snap. Her hurt and anger came spilling out.

"I don't give a damn what you think! I'm not the scared little girl you used to intimidate until she cried. I'm a grown woman. A grown woman who doesn't need your help making her own decisions. A grown woman who can have sex a couple times without becoming someone's"—she made quotation marks in the air—"sweetheart. I don't need a sweetheart. If I did need one, I wouldn't choose a controlling Kingman who treated me like crap for the majority of my life because he was pissed off at my mother. You're still pissed off at my mom. Sooner or later that anger will come out. And I'm through being your scapegoat, Stetson. Now get out of my way!"

She pushed past him and made a mad dash for the door. She expected to be able to breathe once she got outside. But the band around her lungs squeezed even tighter with every step she took. By the time she was heading down the road in her rental car, she was gasping for breath. The breathlessness grew even worse when she looked in the rearview mirror and saw Stetson standing by the cottage watching her leave.

She wanted to head straight to the Dallas airport and get the first available flight to London. But she couldn't leave without saying goodbye to her father and Vivian. All the way into town, she tried to collect herself so her father wouldn't know anything was wrong.

But when he opened the door, he knew immediately. "What happened, Lilliput?"

Her composure crumbled and she fell into his arms. "Oh, Daddy."

# CHAPTER EIGHTEEN

"IT LOOKS TO ME LIKE you're drowning your sorrows." Jasper set the shot of whiskey on the bar in front of Stetson and removed the two empty shot glasses next to it. "And I have to wonder what kind of sorrow a Kingman could possibly have?"

"You should know. You're a Kingman too." Stetson downed the shot.

Jasper grinned. "Oh, but I'm the pauper, not the prince."

"It looks like you're doing all right." He glanced around the crowded bar. "And believe me, you're much luckier not having the responsibility of being Douglas Kingman's oldest son."

"The responsibility of runnin' that big ol' ranch gettin' too much for you, Stet?"

Stetson stared down into his empty shot glass. "It's always been too much for me. I wish I'd inherited a bar that I could sell whenever I wanted and take off for parts unknown."

Jasper set the bottle of whiskey down on the bar. "Anytime you want to change places, cuz, you just let me know." He moved farther down

the bar to take the orders of a couple of old cowboys who had just sat down.

When he was gone, Stetson poured himself
another shot. He had just lifted the glass to his
lips when the door opened and his entire family walked in. Including Adeline. Since his sister
hadn't left the ranch in months, he figured he was
about to catch hell.

He thought about slinking out the side door,
but he didn't have the energy. So he downed
the shot and waited for his family to spot him. It
didn't take long.

"We're supposed to check in with you when
we leave the ranch," Adeline said. "But you don't
have to check in with us?"

He turned on his barstool to face his siblings.
The room spun, and he almost slipped off the
barstool. Wolfe reached out to steady him.

"Whoa there, big brother. It looks like you've
had enough to drink."

"Nope," he said. "I haven't had nearly enough.
So how did you know where to find me?"

"It wasn't hard." Wolfe glanced at Adeline. "I
told you he's upset because Lily left."

"Lily left?" Buck sat down on the barstool next
to Stetson. "Damn, I was hoping to get a chance
with her."

Wolfe cuffed Buck in the back of the head.
"You are dumber than a box of rocks. You never
stood a chance with Lily."

"And you did?"

"No, you idiot. She likes Stetson."

"Wrong-o," Stetson said as he reached for the

bottle of whiskey. "She doesn't like me. I was just a sexual intra-lude. I mean intra-lude."

Delaney sat down on the other side of him and set her cowboy hat on the bar. "I think you mean sexual interlude, Bubba. And what's wrong with that? Why do women always have to want love, marriage, and a baby carriage? Why can't we be like most men and just want a good ol' roll in the hay?"

Stetson wished that's all he'd wanted. But it had never just been about sex with Lily. She'd had him all tangled up with emotions from the moment she first held him.

Delaney propped her elbow on the bar and rested her chin on her fist. "Of course, I can't even get a roll in the hay because every man in this blasted town is a wussy who's too scared of my brothers to give me a little slap and tickle."

"Jesus, Del!" Buck exploded. "TMI! And they better be scared. I don't want just any yahoo messing with my little sister."

"I'm not your little sister. I was born first!"

Buck puffed out his chest. "But you're littler than me."

Delaney rolled her eyes. "Lord, save me from overprotective, dumbass brothers." She looked up and down the bar. "Where did Jasper run off to? I need a strong margarita if I'm going to have to stay here and deal with Buck."

"We're not here to drink, Del," Adeline said. "We're here to make sure Stetson is okay."

"I'm fine, Addie." Stetson was feeling fine. Much better than he'd felt when he first walked in the door of the bar. Then he'd felt like he wanted to hit something. Or cry like a wussy because Lily was gone.

Lily was gone.

Despite his inebriated state, pain speared through his heart. He went to pour himself another shot, but Adeline stopped him.

"You're not fine, Stet. You need to stop drinking and come home."

"I don't want to go home." Home held too many memories of Lily. And right now, she was the last person he wanted to think about. A song by the Zac Brown Band came on the jukebox. The thought of having his toes in the sand was suddenly very appealing. "In fact, I might take a Mexican vacation. I haven't taken a vacation in . . . never. I could use a little time away."

It was an understatement. He needed more than a little time to collect his thoughts and figure out why he felt like he'd been kicked in the stomach by a mule. A month ago, he hadn't cared one way or the other about Lily. But if that were true, then why had he bought all her books and gotten so annoyed every time he read another story about Beetlebub's bullying?

There had always been something about Lily that he felt drawn to. Something he couldn't stay away from. Maybe his bullying hadn't just been because of her mother. Maybe, like any ignorant young boy, he'd been trying to get Lily's attention. And now, just when he'd started to feel like he had it, she had flitted away like one of her fairies, leaving him with an ache in his chest that even whiskey couldn't dull.

"I agree you need a vacation." Adeline took the bottle from him and slid it down the bar. "I'll be happy to help you plan it . . . once we get home."

"Why does Stet get a vacation and the rest of us don't?" Buck complained. "I work just as hard. I could use a trip to Mexico too."

"Just shut up, Buck," Delaney snapped. "Everything isn't always about you."

Before Buck could snap back, Adeline held up a hand. "Delaney is right. You had your time to run wild after college. Stetson never did. He was always taking care of the ranch and us. Now it's time we returned the favor." She took Stetson's arm. "Come on, big brother. Let's go home."

Stetson shook his head and refused to budge. "Not yet, Addie."

She sighed and sent Buck and Wolfe a look. Without her having to say a word, they each grabbed one of Stetson's arms.

"Let me go," he growled. "I'm still the boss."

"Sorry," Wolfe said as he pulled him off the bar stool. "But you're only the boss when you're sober and not lovesick."

Lovesick? He wanted to argue, but the pain in his heart wouldn't let him. He was lovesick. He was a lovesick mess, and that pissed him off as much as his brothers forcing him out the door of the bar. He waited until they were in the parking lot before he elbowed Wolfe in the stomach and shoved Buck on his butt.

The fight was on.

Both his brothers charged him. He still held his

own . . . until Wolfe's fist connected with his jaw. Then Stetson went down for the count.

He woke up in the passenger seat of his truck. He flexed his jaw and grimaced as he stared out the windshield at the pouring rain. Adeline was driving. While she was prim and proper about everything else, she drove like a Nascar driver on the final lap. Usually, he was scared to death to drive with her. Especially when it was raining. But tonight, he only leaned back in the seat and closed his eyes. The alcohol was starting to wear off, and he felt like shit. His jaw hurt where Wolfe had hit him, but that was nothing compared to his aching heart.

"So Wolfe was right," Adeline said. "You've fallen in love with Lily Daltry."

He wanted to deny it, but he couldn't when his chest felt like a hollow void. He loved Lily. But it made no difference now. She was gone. Long gone.

As if reading his thoughts, Adeline sighed. "I was worried about you getting hurt. You've always had a problem staying away from Lily. Even when you were little, you were infatuated with her." He was surprised his sister had known something he'd just figured out. "You sought Lily out every chance you got," Adeline continued. "Even if it was to be mean to her. Why were you so mean?"

He didn't know if it was the alcohol or his pain that made him blurt out the truth. "Because I wanted to make her pay." And now he was pay-ing. Fate had balanced the scales with notes in a teapot. He'd made Lily pay for something that wasn't her fault. Now Lily was making him pay for something that wasn't his.

Adeline turned to him. "Make her pay? Please tell me you weren't mean to Lily because you wanted to get back at her mother for having an affair with Daddy."

Stetson sat up and stared at his sister. "You knew?"

Adeline laughed. "You and our brothers think I'm so innocent. But I have eyes, Stet. And Daddy was horrible at hiding his affairs."

"Affairs? He had more than one?"

She shot a look of disbelief at him. "Now who's the innocent? Everyone in town knew about Daddy's affairs."

Stetson shook his head. "I didn't. I thought he'd only had an affair with Gwen." He stared at the rain hitting the windshield. "All these years, I thought she was the one who led our father astray."

Adeline snorted. "Then you didn't know Daddy very well. Like Wolfe, he loved women. All women. And I think he thought he had the right after Grandpa King forced him into marriage with Mama."

"So he really didn't love her." All these years, Stetson had hoped he was wrong.

"I thought the same thing," Adeline said. "But if he didn't love her, why was he so devastated when she died?"

"Because he blamed himself. The night Mama died, I heard them arguing. She had found out about his affair with Gwen."

Adeline shot him a shocked look. "Oh my God. Why didn't you tell me?"

"You were too young to know. Hell, I was too young to know. My brain couldn't comprehend what was happening. All I knew was that Daddy and Mama were fighting because Daddy loved Lily's mom and it upset Mama so much she left the house . . . and never came back."

Adeline returned her gaze to the highway. "So that's why you and Daddy never got along after Mama passed."

It was a harsh truth that was hard to swallow. He had let the events of one night affect his relationship with his father. All because he blamed him for his mother's death. But it hadn't been Douglas's fault. Or Gwen's. His mom's death had just been a horrible accident. Blaming people hadn't brought her back. All it had done was turn Stetson into a vengeful fool in search of justice. Which made him no better than whoever was currently causing all the problems on the ranch. Stetson might not have burned down a barn or carved up an animal. But he had burned the bridge of reconciliation with his father and carved up his father's heart.

And, in the process, his own.

He closed his eyes and leaned his head back on the seat. "Lily is right. I haven't been able to let go of the past. No wonder she wasn't willing to stay. How can she trust that we could work things out when I've let Daddy's affair with her mama affect my entire life?"

"So she knows about her mom and Daddy?"

He nodded. "She just found out."

"That must've been a horrible shock for her. Especially since she and her mother were so close." She glanced over at him. "Maybe her leaving has nothing to do with you, Stet. Maybe she just needs some time to process everything."

It was pathetic how quickly he latched on to Adeline's theory. But it did make sense. It had taken Stetson years to get over his father's affair with Gwen . . . and he'd expected Lily to deal with it in minutes. He'd charged into the bedroom and tried to force her to stay. No wonder she'd exploded and run off. She hadn't needed a control freak. She had just needed someone to understand what she was going through and back off.

Maybe if he gave her some time, Lily would be willing to give him another chance. Maybe if he could prove to her that he had left the past where it belonged, they could start over. No expectations. No pressure. Just two old friends talking on the phone or exchanging texts. In fact, maybe he should text her now. Nothing lengthy. Just a simple . . .

*I miss you.*

The squeal of tires pulled him from his thoughts, and he suddenly realized how fast they were going.

"Dammit, Addie," he snapped. "Slow down!"

She took the sharp curve on two tires. "I'm trying to slow down. Something's wrong with the brakes. They aren't working."

Stetson stared out the windshield at the rain-slick highway. If they hadn't been on an incline and going so fast, he would've told her to pull the emergency brake. But stopping too fast now could cause them to spin out.

He grabbed onto the dashboard. "Just keep control until we get off this winding hill, then—watch out!" A mule deer jumped out in front of the truck. Adeline swerved and missed the deer, but the sudden swerve caused the tires to skid and the truck to go into a spin.

Stetson reached out an arm to protect Adeline. But when the truck hit something and rolled, he knew there was no protecting his sister.

Or himself.

All he could do was pray.

# CHAPTER NINETEEN

"WHY, YOU'VE ONLY TAKEN A few bites of your pancakes," Thelma Davenport said as she refilled Lily's coffee mug. "You used to eat your weight in Otis's pancakes when you were a little girl. Don't tell me you're on a diet. Not when you're such a little bitty thing."

"I'm just not very hungry this morning," Lily said. She hadn't wanted to come to Good Eats for breakfast, but her father had insisted she eat something before she left for the airport. She knew he was worried about her. He sat in the booth across from her, watching her with concerned eyes as Thelma refilled his cup.

"Well, if y'all need anything else, you just let me know." Thelma winked at Lily. "Soda crackers and ginger ale always worked for me when I was expecting."

Lily stared at her with shock. "Expecting? I'm not pregnant."

Thelma blinked. "You're not? But Kitty told everyone at the last Cursed Ladies' Auxiliary meeting that Stetson took you to a doctor's appointment the other day. The only time a man goes with a woman to a doctor's appointment is when she's pregnant or has a life-threatening disease." Her brown eyes widened. "You aren't sick, are you? You do look a little pale."

Lily shook her head. "I'm fine." Or she would be once she got back to England. "Stetson didn't take me to a doctor's appointment. He took me to the elementary school to talk to Vivian's class about writing."

Thelma looked thoroughly disappointed. "Well, that's a shame. All the Cursed Ladies agree that you and Stetson will make cute babies."

It was a struggle to keep her emotions in check. "Stetson and I aren't a couple."

Thelma eyes widened. "You're not? But at the wedding, it looked like you two were . . ." She waved a hand. "Never mind. You just let me know if y'all need anything else."

When she was gone, her father chuckled. "Small town gossip." He looked at Lily and his smile faded. "But she's right. You do look pale."

"I'm fine, Daddy. Really." If she kept saying it, maybe it would become reality. She checked the time on her phone. "I need to go. I don't want to miss my plane." But before she could slide out of the booth, her father stopped her.

"We need to talk, Lilliput." When she settled back in her seat, he heaved a deep sigh. "You and I both know I'm not a good parent." She started to argue, but he held up a hand. "Don't try to deny the truth. I never felt comfortable being a dad. Which is why I let your mother do most of the parenting. I regret that. I am your parent.

Your only parent. Comfortable with it or not, it's about damned time I started acting like it." He paused. "I didn't fall for that cock-and-bull story you gave me last night about being so weepy over leaving the cottage. So while Vivian was getting you settled in the spare room, I headed out to the ranch to have a little chat with Stetson."

Lily's eyes widened. "You didn't."

"I sure as hell did. You're my baby girl. If someone makes you cry, they're going to answer to me."

"What did you do, Daddy?"

"I planned to punch Stetson in the nose. But he wasn't at the ranch house. When I stopped by the cottage to see if he was there, I realized it wasn't Stetson that had you so upset. It was the notes you left on the kitchen island."

Lily's heart plummeted. She had been so distraught she hadn't even thought about destroying the evidence of her mother's affair. Now her father knew, and she was to blame.

"I'm so sorry, Daddy." She reached across the table and took his hand. "I didn't want you to find out."

He gave her fingers a gentle squeeze. "I didn't find out from the notes, Lilliput. I knew long before last night about your mother's affair with Douglas Kingman. She confessed everything to me."

Lily stared at him. "Why didn't you ever tell me?"

"Because she was your mother. I didn't want to taint your memories of her. It was a mistake she regretted. Your mother loved me. I've never doubted that. Yes, she had an affair. But I understand why. She was in a brand-new country and was feeling a little out of place. Along came Douglas Kingman. He was a lot like Wolfe. He knew how to make a woman feel special and needed." He shook his head. "Something that doesn't come easy to me. Your mother fell for his charm, but she also realized her mistake and was sorry about it."

Lily didn't know how to feel. One part of her was still resentful about her mother's betrayal. But the other part was proud of her mother for the bravery it had taken to confess to Theo and try to make amends.

"I can understand why you stayed with Mum," she said. "But knowing that she and Douglas had an affair, why did you stay at the ranch? How could you continue to work for a man who had an affair with your wife?"

"We had signed a contract with King, and we'd have been in breach of that contract if we didn't finish the job. Plus, we had already uprooted you from England. Your mother and I didn't want to uproot you again. Still, we might've left when the garden was finished if Elizabeth Kingman hadn't died in that horrible accident. One night a few days after the funeral, Douglas showed up at the cottage and completely broke down. He felt like God was punishing him for not loving his wife by taking her. As he cried and confessed all his wrongdoings, your mother and I realized that if anyone needed a friend, Douglas Kingman did."

"So you just forgave him?"

He smiled. "People make mistakes, Lilliput. If we can't forgive and forget, then how can we expect our loved ones to forgive and forget our mistakes?"

"I don't think you've ever made a mistake in your life, Daddy."

He patted her hand. "Well, thanks for thinking so highly of me, honey. But I've made plenty. One was not being a better father to you. I should've spent more time with you. I shouldn't have left all the parenting to Gwen just because she was so much better at it than I was."

Her mother had been a good parent. The best parent. Lily had been about to let a mistake made years before erase all the good memories. Just like she had let her grief erase them. She'd run away and hidden in England. Come to think of it, running away and hiding had always been her forte.

Her father glanced at his watch. "Now you better get going or you're going to miss your plane." When he looked back at her, his eyes held tears. "I'm going to miss you, Lilliput. I had hoped your visit might make you realize how much you missed home. But I guess this isn't your home anymore. Vivian said that writers like you need to live in a place that inspires you. I figure Cursed isn't it. You haven't written at all while you've been here."

"It's not that, Daddy. I can't write in England either." She took a deep breath and stopped running from the truth. "I've run out of Mum's stories."

He squinted at her. "What do you mean?"

"The fairy stories aren't mine. They're Mum's. I just drew the pictures that went with them. And now that I've run out of the stories she told me, I'm struggling to write another one. My editor is expecting the new book in less than a month and I haven't written a word. Not one word."

She expected her father to be shocked speechless. Or to give her a lecture on how disappointed he was in her for plagiarizing her mother's stories. She did not expect him to think she'd lost her mind.

"I'm sorry, but that's the craziest thing I've ever heard. Of course you wrote those stories. Your mother might've given you the idea, but the Fairy Prairie stories I read were nothing like the stories your mother told you."

"You heard the stories Mum told me?"

"Not all of them, but enough to know they were just simple stories she made up to keep her daughter entertained while we worked in the garden. Her fairies had wings and were magical, but that's about the end of the similarities. Her fairies didn't tame dragonflies or rope beetles. They didn't live on a Texas prairie and play tricks on unsuspecting cowboys. Nor did they deal with the issues that your fairies deal with. They didn't struggle to make friends. Or get scared of the dark. Or deal with bullies. They just flitted around having fun. You brought her fairies to life—not just by drawing them, but also by giving them human traits and personalities and problems that kids can relate to."

Lily felt completely blindsided. Was her father right? She scrambled through her mind trying to remember the stories her mother had told her. But all she could come up with were images of kneeling next to her mother in the dirt while Gwen spoke in her soft, loving voice. The exact words weren't clear. And Lily realized they never had been. She had just remembered the moments they'd shared. The love and security she'd felt building a fairy garden or planting a flower or swinging in the hammock. She put those feelings into what she could remember of the stories and turned them into Fairy Prairie. She had always believed it was her mother's stories she was writing down, but now she realized her mother had only given her the framework for her stories. Lily was the one who had filled in all the details.

She stared at her father. "I *did* write the stories."

"You sure did." He grinned. "Although you might've had a little help from the Kingmans."

Lily laughed. "And here I'd thought I did such a good job of disguising the Kingmans in fairy wings. But even Stetson recognized himself."

Her father's smile faded. "Do you still think he's a bully?"

It was a good question. She didn't hesitate to answer it. "No. Like you said, he's a good man."

"If that's true, why are you leaving? He cares about you, Lilliput. I think you care about him too."

"I do. But he can't forget the past. Which means we don't have a future."

"Stetson said that?"

"He didn't have to. I've experienced firsthand the grudge he held against Mum. He didn't like me when we were kids because he found out about her affair with his father."

Her father's eyes turned sad. "Poor kid. You know how hard finding out about the affair has been on you, and you're an adult. As a kid, it must've been twice as hard on Stetson. So I get why he held a grudge. But he doesn't seem to be holding a grudge against you anymore. You can't expect him to forget the past. No one forgets the past. I didn't forget your mother's affair. But I loved her enough not to let it ruin what we had together. I'll never forget the times I had with your mother, but that's not going to stop me from having just as much fun with Vivian. We don't need to forget the past, but we do need to live in the present. Now the question is, who do you want to spend this present moment with, Lilliput?"

Only one word came out of her mouth. "Stetson."

When her father gave her a long, hard look, she realized what she needed to do. She picked up her phone and cancelled her flight. The relief that flooded her was a good indication she'd made the right decision. So was the wide smile on her father's face. She wanted to call Stetson. But she wasn't about to have an intimate conversation in front of her dad. Besides, she needed to apologize to Stetson in person. She had said some hateful things to him before she'd left the ranch and she wanted to look in his beautiful brown eyes when she told him how sorry she was.

There was also something else she needed to tell him.

But before she could wave at Thelma for the check, the door of the diner swung open and Kitty Carson hustled in with her mailbag slung over her shoulder. Her large boobs bounced as she hurried over to the counter and took a seat at the bar.

"Give me your strongest cup of coffee, Thelma." She waved her hand in front of her flushed cheeks. "Lord, have I got some sad news for you. I just ran into Dalhart Kerns at the gas station, and he told me that his cousin—you know the one who looks like Elmer Fudd and owns that old junkyard off of Highway 10—called him this morning and told him a truck was towed to his junkyard late last night that had been in a major accident. He said it was as flat as a stomped Coke can. And you'll never guess who the truck belonged to." She leaned in closer and whispered something to Thelma.

Whatever she whispered had Thelma pulling back in shock and holding a hand to her chest. "Lord have mercy. First, his mama dies in a car accident and now he does."

Lily stared at the two women as her heart seemed to fall right out of her chest. As if in a dream, she got up and walked toward Kitty. "Whose truck was it, Kitty?"

Kitty drew back in surprise. "Why, Lily Daltry. I didn't see—"

"Whose truck!" Lily yelled louder than she had

ever yelled in her life and both Thelma and Kitty drew back at her outburst.

"It was Stetson Kingman's." Kitty's eyes filled with tears. "A cryin' shame. Such a cryin' shame."

Lily turned and headed for the door, but her father caught up to her before she could reach her car.

"Calm down, Lily. You know Kitty rarely gets her facts straight."

She turned to him. "But what if she's right?"

"Then we'll deal with it as it comes." He took out his cell phone. "We need to call the King-mans and find out what's going on."

It seemed like it took forever for her father to make the call. The entire time, Lily stood there with her heart beating out of her chest and tears streaming down her cheeks.

Stetson couldn't be dead. He just couldn't be.

When someone answered, Lily held her breath as her father asked about Stetson. The look on his face said it all.

"And you don't have any more details?" he asked. "Okay, then. Thank you." He lowered his phone and looked at Lily. "It was Stetson's truck, but—" Before he could finish, Lily's knees gave out. Her father caught her before she hit the ground. He held her close. "He's alive, Lily. Both he and Adeline are alive. They're at the county hospital."

"I have to see him," she said. "I have to tell him I'm sorry. And I have to tell him that I love him." There was no doubt in her mind now. She loved Stetson.

Her patted her back. "Okay, Lilliput. I'll get you to Stetson."

Theo had always followed the speed limit, but he drove well over it on the way to the hospital. As he drove, Lily prayed. If God would just let him live, she'd start living too. She wouldn't hide in her stories anymore. She'd start experiencing life for herself. She wanted that life to be with Stetson. She realized that now.

Once they reached the hospital, her tears had dried. But fear still clenched her stomach as her father checked in at the front desk. Lily relaxed a little when the woman gave them a room number. If Stetson was in a regular room, he had to be okay. When she stepped into the room and saw him, her fear returned. There was a huge bandage on his forehead, his face was puffy and bruised, and one eye was swollen shut. He was hooked up to all kinds of IVs and monitors.

"Stetson," she whispered.

He turned to her. His one eye widened. "You didn't go."

She walked over to the bed on wobbly legs. Her smile was just as wobbly. "How could I leave when everyone I love is right here? I'm so sorry. I shouldn't have exploded like I did and said all those hurtful things."

"No, I'm the one who's sorry. I was an idiot—I've been an idiot for a long time."

Delaney got up from the chair in the corner. "And I'm sorry that I have to sit here and witness this mushy scene. If y'all will excuse me, I'm going to go check on Adeline and make sure our overprotective brothers aren't driving her to drink like they do me." She walked over to hug Stetson, but he held up a hand.

"Thanks, Del, but your last hug almost broke a rib."

"Suck it up, wuss," she said as she leaned over to hug him. But Lily noticed she was careful and there were tears in her eyes as she whispered. "I love you, Bubba." She straightened with a sniff and turned to Lily. "Don't give him too much pity, Lily, or he'll become soft like Buck."

As Delaney headed out the door, Theo excused himself too. "I think I'll go check on Addie as well."

Once Delaney and her father were gone, Lily turned to Stetson. He looked so battered that it broke her heart. "How do you feel?"

"Like I rolled over in a truck. But I feel much better now that you're here."

She moved closer and smoothed a strand of hair off his forehead. "Can I get you anything?"

He took her hand and attempted a smile. "I have all I need. But there is something I'd like you to clarify. When you said that everyone you loved was here—was I included in that everyone? Do you love me, Lily Daltry?"

Tears filled her eyes as she nodded. "I love you, Stetson Kingman."

He closed his eye and sighed. "Well, that's good. Because I love you too. I love you so much that when you left, I thought I was going to go crazy."

"I was feeling a little crazy myself when I thought you were . . ." Tears clogged her throat and she couldn't finish.

"Aww, baby." Stetson scooted over and tried to pull her into bed with him, but she drew back.

"I'll hurt you."

"You'll hurt me more if you don't get in this bed right now." He gave her a beseeching look. "I need you to hold me, Lily."

There was no way she could deny him. Not when she needed to be held too. She carefully climbed into the bed and settled against his chest. The steady thump of his heart was the best sound she'd ever heard in her life. He sighed as if he was just as content. They remained that way for a long time. Finally, Stetson spoke.

"Tell me a story, Lily."

She smiled. "What kind of story?"

"A fairy story, of course."

Lily had thought she had run out of stories because she couldn't remember any more of her mother's. But now she realized she'd run out of stories because she had nothing going on in her life to fuel her imagination. She hadn't been making memories in England. She'd just been trying to forget the memories she'd made. But they'd refused to be forgotten and had surfaced in her stories. When she'd run out of memories, she'd run out of stories. Now that she was back where she belonged, she had made more than enough memories to spark her imagination.

"Once upon a time, there was a shy little fairy named Poppy," she began. "And Poppy was afraid of most everything. She had taken to hiding in her garden and living in her wild imagination instead of living in the real world. But another fairy, named Beetlebub, refused to let her live in her dream world. For years, she viewed him as a mean nasty bully. But one day, while looking for her father, she flew into Beetlebub's lair."

"Made of spider webs," Stetson added.

She laughed. "Yes, made of spider webs. Poor Poppy got trapped in the sticky web. She thought for certain she'd be eaten by Beetlebub's pet spiders. Or by the beastly fairy himself. But instead, she got to know the fairy behind the scars. She discovered Beetlebub wasn't the beast she thought he was. He was really a hero who loved his family and worked hard to do right by them and all the fairies on Fairy Prairie. She fell madly in love with Beetlebub." She cuddled closer to Stetson. "They lived happily ever after."

Stetson stiffened. "Wait a minute. That was the end? It can't just end like that."

She laughed. "Hey, it's my story. I get to choose how it ends."

"Fine. Then I'll tell my own story." He took a few minutes before he spoke. "Once upon a time, there was this idiot Beetlebub who let past hurt turn him into a big ol' bully. Especially with this cute little fairy named Poppy. One night, he told her all about why he was so hurt. And you know what that smart fairy did? Why she healed him with a hug. What Beetlebub didn't know was that the hug was magic. It made him fall in love with Poppy. From that day on, he followed her around Fairy Prairie like a lovesick fairy. He knew there was only one thing to do."

When he didn't say anything, Lily lifted her head and looked at him. "What was that?"

His gaze locked with hers. "Let go of the past and marry the woman he loves."

Lily's heart started to beat overtime. "You want me to marry you?"

"More than anything in the world. What do you say, Lily?"

It had taken her a while to find her happily-ever-after. She wasn't about to let it slip through her fingers. "Yes."

Stetson smiled, showing off his dimple. "Now that's the proper way to end a story."

# CHAPTER TWENTY

STETSON STOOD IN HIS BEDROOM look-ing out the window at the garden that looked like a giant fairyland. Hundreds of lights had been added to every tree and shrub and they twin-kled like a Texas sky at midnight. White clothed tables with their own fairy garden centerpieces had been set up in the English rose garden and a dance floor had been set up beneath the old oak that was filled with colorful lanterns. When the May breeze caused the lanterns to sway, dots of colored light danced among the leaves like mag-ical fairies.

Maybe fairies were dancing in the tree tonight. Lily said fairies were drawn to parties. A few months ago, Stetson would have scoffed at the fanciful idea. But not anymore. Now, the entire world felt like it was filled with magic. He truly believed God had sent him a special fairy to take him out of his dreary life and make him believe again.

A knock sounded on the door, pulling him out of his musings. He answered it and found Gage standing there in a dusty black cowboy hat, a soft-looking chambray shirt, faded jeans, and worn-in cowboy boots. Stetson would've loved to swap clothes with him. The tuxedos Adeline had insisted Stetson and his brothers wear were damn uncomfortable. But since Addie had worked so hard on turning the garden into Lily's fantasy, Stetson hadn't argued. He wasn't going to complain about it now. He hadn't asked Gage to come to his room to talk about uncomfortable tuxedos.

Stetson motioned him in. "Have you stationed cowboys all around the perimeter of the garden? Including the labyrinth where the ceremony is going to take place?"

"Yes, sir, Boss. Everyone's in position with radios in hand to contact me if there's anything suspicious. Did you hear back from the private investigator you hired about the prints he found on your truck hood?"

After Sheriff Dobbs had ignored Stetson's insistence that his truck's brakes had been tampered with, Stetson had hired his own investigator to look into things. Unfortunately, after weeks of looking, he hadn't found anything. But Stetson wasn't going to give up. He'd hire as many investigators as it took to find the man responsible for almost killing Adeline. And him.

"The prints belonged to Dalhart's cousin at the junkyard," Stetson said. "He no doubt was messing around the truck trying to figure out who it belonged to." He shook his head. "The sheriff should've dusted for prints before he let the tow truck take it."

"Dobbs is worthless," Gage said. "It's too bad Nasty Jack's doesn't have surveillance cameras."

"My uncle Jack is too cheap for that. But at least we know it was someone at the bar that night. Someone who has access to the ranch. That should narrow our search down. The investigator has talked to Jasper and they're compiling a list. I was hoping he'd find something before Lily and I left for England. Since he hasn't, I'm thinking it might be best if we canceled our flights."

"Now, Boss, I realize you're worried about your family, but I don't think canceling your honeymoon is the best way to start your marriage."

"Canceling your honeymoon?" Adeline walked into the room. Like Stetson, her bruises had faded. But she still wore a cast on her arm. The sling didn't take away from how pretty she looked in the soft lavender maid of honor gown.

Pretty but angry.

"There's no way you're going to cancel your trip, Stetson Douglas. Not only because you need to help Lily pack up her home, but also because you deserve a vacation. If I have to drive you to the airport and force you on the plane, you're going to get one. That's final."

Stetson couldn't help but smile. It was good to see the spark of life in his sister's eyes. Even if it was an angry spark directed at him. But he still worried about leaving the ranch.

"I'll take a vacation. I'm just thinking it might be best if Lily and I waited until—"

Adeline cut in. "No waiting. I know you, Stet. If you put it off now, you'll find some other excuse for not going. I realize you're worried about all of us after what happened, but we're not kids anymore. We'll be fine."

Before Stetson could continue to argue, Gage jumped in. "Don't worry, Boss. I plan to keep a close eye on everyone."

Adeline turned on Gage with flashing eyes. "You don't need to keep an eye on me, Mr. Reardon."

Gage studied Adeline for a long moment before he turned to Stetson. "I'll talk to you later, Boss."

Once he was gone, Stetson chuckled. "Quit terrorizing the poor man, Addie."

She continued to look at the doorway Gage had walked out of. "I seriously doubt that man is scared of anything." She looked back at Stetson. "Similar to you."

"I'm scared of things. Lily for one." He paused. "And my family getting hurt for another. I don't like leaving when a madman is on the loose."

Adeline sighed. "You can't keep us from getting hurt, Stet. You couldn't stop the truck accident. Or Daddy fooling around with every woman in town. Or our parents dying." She paused. "Or Danny. Bad things happen in life. It's just the way it is. So stop carrying us, big brother. We can walk on our own."

It was easier said than done. He'd been watching out for his siblings for so long, it was hard to let go and trust they could do just fine on their own. As if reading his thoughts, Adeline walked over and straightened his bowtie.

"We'll be okay, Stet. You're starting a new life

with a special woman today. Enjoy it. Enjoy every second you and Lily have together." She finished with his bowtie and looked up at him. "I love you."

"Aww, Addie." He pulled her into his arms. "I love you too. Thank you for making this day so special. The garden looks just like fairies would play there."

"I hope to see a lot of little fairies playing there one day." She drew back. "I'm thrilled you and Lily have decided to move into the cottage. I think it's time my big brother moved out."

"You're not worried about having to deal with all the sibling bickering alone?"

"I think I can handle it."

As hard as it was, he realized it was time to let Adeline prove it. "Don't let Buck and Delaney kill each other while I'm gone. And make sure you and Delaney don't go anywhere without Buck or Wolfe."

"I don't need Buck or Wolfe following me around!" Delaney strode into the room. She wore a similar dress to Adeline's. But instead of heels, she wore scuffed cowboy boots that looked like she'd worn them to muck out the stalls. "I mean it, Stet. I'm just as strong and good with a gun as Buck and Wolfe."

"Like hell you are." Buck followed behind Delaney. "And anytime you want me to prove it, you just let me know, little sister."

Delaney whirled on him. "I'm not your little—"

"Give it a rest, Del." Wolfe walked into the

room. While Buck looked as uncomfortable in his tuxedo as Stetson did, Wolfe looked completely at ease. He flopped down on Stetson's bed and reclined back on the pillows, crossing his black polished boots at the ankle. "You sure you want to be stuck with one woman forever, Stet? Especially when there are so many female fish in the sea?"

"One day, you'll learn, Wolfe, that being caught by the right person is as close to heaven as you can get." Stetson shoved Wolfe's feet off the bed. "And get your damned boots off my bed."

Wolfe sat up. "If getting married is heaven, I think I would prefer hell."

"Of course you would." Lily swept into the room. Stetson forgot to breathe. She looked like a vision in the frothy white wedding gown with her dark curls piled up on her head and soft tendrils falling around her beautiful features. Before Stetson could tell her how stunning she looked, Adeline cut in.

"What are you doing, Lily? Stetson's not supposed to see you before the wedding. It's bad luck."

Lily shrugged her bare shoulders . . . that Stetson really wanted to run his lips over. "I wanted to make sure the groom hasn't gotten cold feet." She glared at Wolfe. "Or his brother wasn't giving him cold feet."

Wolfe held up his hands. "Now, I was just making sure, Lily. And it seems my brother can't wait to be shackled to you."

Lily arched an eyebrow and tapped her foot.

"Shackled?"

"What my idiot brother is trying to say," Delaney said. "Is that Stetson's feet are as toasty as burnt marshmallows."

Buck moved closer to Lily. "And if he does get cold feet, I'll be more than happy to take his place."

Wolfe got up from the bed and shoved Buck. "Would you shut up?"

"Hey!" Buck shoved Wolfe and he stumbled into Delaney, who shoved him back into Buck. Adeline hurried to corral her siblings.

"Stop it right now."

But they didn't pay Adeline the least bit of attention. Stetson was about to get involved when Lily spoke in a loud, authoritative voice.

"That's enough!"

Buck, Wolfe, and Delaney stopped shoving and turned to Lily who started issuing orders like a drill sergeant. "Buck, you need to find Jasper and get down to the garden to help seat the guests. Wolfe, go get your tuxedo jacket on and make sure you have the ring I gave you earlier. If you've lost it, I'm going to box your ears. Delaney, I realize you hate the high heels I bought you, but please wipe the manure off your boots. And Adeline, would you mind checking with Potts and making sure the enchiladas and tacos are ready for the reception?"

Stetson's four siblings followed her bidding much faster than they had ever followed his. Once they were gone, Stetson did what he'd been wanting to do since Lily had walked in the room. He pulled her into his arms. After a thorough kiss, he drew back and smiled.

"I was worried you couldn't handle my family, but it looks like you're going to be just fine."

"Of course I am. I can handle Kingmans."

He bent his head and kissed his way along her neck. "You sure can." She sighed and wrapped her arms around him. Something sharp poked him in the neck. He drew back. "Oww. What's that?"

Lily dropped her arms. "Oh baby, I'm sorry. I forgot about Beetlebub." She held up a tiny fairy doll with black wings, a ferocious look, and a rose thorn clutched in his fist. At Stetson's surprised look, Lily laughed. "I just received prototypes of the Fairy Prairie dolls this morning. Meet Beetlebub." She held up her other hand that held a girl fairy with delicate wings, long ebony hair, and a shy smile. "And Poppy. Aren't they cute?"

Stetson could see how excited she was and he didn't want to burst her bubble, but . . . "I wouldn't call Beetlebub cute. He looks pissed. And why is he clutching that rose thorn like he plans to stab someone with it?"

Lily turned the doll to look at it. "He's not pissed. He's . . . stern. And I'm not sure why they gave him a weapon. I guess it makes him more of a fighting action figure. See." She pushed a button on the back of the doll and Beetlebub's arm jerked up and down in a slashing motion.

"That's horrible. I'm not a thorn–wielding killer."

"They're just toys, Stetson." She tossed the

dolls onto his bed. "Beetlebub isn't you. Just like Poppy isn't me." When he cocked an eyebrow, she conceded. "Okay, so I thought I was using us as templates for my fairies. But it turned out I was completely wrong. I didn't know who you really are. And I certainly didn't know who I really am. But now I know you're not an angry bully and I'm not a shy little girl scared of her own shadow. In the next Fairy Prairie book, Beetlebub and Poppy figure out who they truly are—a sweet, responsible fairy who takes care of his own and a talented, strong fairy who learns how to speak her mind."

He stared at her. "You finished the book?"

She grinned and nodded. "I sent if off to my publishers this morning."

"And do Beetlebub and Poppy get a happy ending?"

"Nope."

His eyes widened. "No?"

She looped her arms around his neck. "This isn't the ending for Beetlebub and Poppy. They have a lot more adventures to go on." She smiled and lit up his world. "A lot more."

## THE END

*Turn the page for a special SNEAK PEEK of the next Kingman Ranch novel!*

SNEAK PEEK!
# *Charming a Knight in Cowboy Boots*
coming April 2022

B E CAREFUL WHAT YOU WISH for.
      Adeline Raquel Kingman hadn't followed
this golden rule, and subsequently, she was des-
tined to live her life regretting it. Wishes held
power. More power than she had ever imagined. Once she'd realized that, it was too late.
Her wishes had already been granted . . . in the
worst possible ways. Now she was careful not to
wish for anything. She didn't blow out birthday
candles, break wishbones, care if the clock read
11:11, carefully pick up fallen eyelashes, notice
rainbows . . . or toss pennies into fountains.

She looked down at the coins that littered the
bottom of the fountain her grandfather, "King"
Kingman, had shipped across the Atlantic for his
garden. Beneath the moonlit water, the pennies,
nickels, dimes, and quarters glittered like sunken
treasure. Like sunken treasure, some coins were
cursed. Or at least, Adeline's were. If she knew
which coins were hers, she'd jump into the fountain and reclaim her wishes.

But it wouldn't turn back time.

It wouldn't bring back her mother and father. Or Danny.

A wave of tiredness washed over her. She was used to the feeling. She hadn't slept well in months and usually felt exhausted and drained. It took a real effort to get through each day. But she did. Not for herself, but for her three brothers and sister. If it were up to Adeline, she would continue to hide away in her tower room. But she couldn't do that to Stetson, Wolfe, Delaney, and Buck. They had been through enough without having to worry about her.

Still, it was exhausting to pretend everything was all right when everything felt all wrong. It had taken all her energy to smile and greet guests at Stetson's wedding reception. Which was why she had escaped and was hiding in the hedge labyrinth. She'd thought if she just had a few minutes alone to collect herself, she would be able to continue the farce. But now she felt even more drained. Like a flower devoid of water and sunlight.

She lay back on the cold stone ledge that ran along the fountain, resting her casted arm across her stomach. If she could just take a short catnap, maybe she would have enough energy to make it through the reception. Just five minutes of sleep was all she needed. Just five short minutes of oblivion with no memories or guilt.

Was that too much to ask?

She closed her eyes. But just as the fog of oblivion descended, she was pulled back to harsh reality.

"Miss Kingman."

She opened her eyes and turned her head. She could just make out the shape of a cowboy in the shadows. His broad shoulders filled the opening between the hedges and the crown of his hat almost reached the top of the high, neatly trimmed shrubs.

There was only one ranch hand that big.

Exhaustion was replaced with a surge of wakefulness. She popped up and tried to act like sleeping on a fountain ledge during a wedding reception was a completely normal thing to do.

"Yes, Mr. Reardon? What did you need?"

Gage Reardon's large, shadowy form didn't move. Or speak. He rarely spoke to her. He always directed his comments or replies to her brother, Stetson. Stetson found it amusing that Adeline's beauty left Gage flustered. She didn't agree. Gage wasn't the type of man who got flustered. He just didn't think she was worthy of his attention.

Which annoyed her.

"Did you hear me, Mr. Reardon?" she asked. "Or do you need my brother here to translate?"

She could feel his hard gaze, and it was a struggle not to fidget beneath it. Finally, after what felt like forever, he spoke. "You shouldn't be out here all by yourself, Miss Kingman. You need to get back to the party."

She knew he was just following orders. Stetson's orders. Ever since the accident, Adeline had not been allowed to do anything alone. If her three brothers weren't keeping watch over her, this man was. And she was sick of it. She wasn't a sheep who needed a shepherd.

She stood and shook the wrinkles out of her lavender maid of honor gown. "I realize you're Stetson's right hand man. But you don't give me orders, Mr. Reardon. I'll go back to the reception when I want to go back to the reception." She waited for him to leave.

Unfortunately, he didn't. He just continued to stand there as still as the bronze horse statues that were placed throughout the garden.

She crossed her arms to show her annoyance—which was difficult with her cast. "Is there something else you needed, Mr. Reardon?"

"No, ma'am."

"Then why are you still here?"

There was another long pause. "Because you are."

She dropped her arms. "So you aren't going to leave until I do?"

"Pretty much."

Now thoroughly ticked, she took a few steps closer. "I'm ordering you to leave, Mr. Reardon."

"I don't take my orders from you, Miss Kingman. I take them from your brother. And he's asked me to keep an eye on his family. You included. I won't have something happening to you on my watch." His cowboy hat dipped, and she knew he looked at her cast. "You should understand that after what happened to you and Stetson."

She huffed out her breath. "Believe me, I do understand, but I doubt seriously that whoever tampered with the brakes on Stetson's truck and caused our accident is stupid enough to try something in the middle of a wedding reception attended by the entire town."

"What makes you think that would be stupid?"

"Because he'd be caught. All I have to do is scream and my brothers—"

For a large man, Gage moved quickly. Before Adeline realized what was happening, he had a hand over her mouth and her pinned against his rock solid body.

Adeline suddenly felt like she had been plugged into a power source. A sizzling current raced through her, obliterating her exhaustion. After months of feeling absolutely nothing, she felt. She felt her heart thumping madly beneath her ribcage. Blood racing through her veins. Her lungs expanding with every breath. And her nerves tingling on every square inch of her skin.

She was terrified.

Not of Gage. She knew he was just trying to prove a point. She felt terrified of all the feelings that seemed to be gushing up from the vault she'd locked them in. She felt like she hadn't felt since before Danny died—or possibly even before that. And she didn't want to feel. It was much better not to. But when Gage spoke close to her ear, his deep voice with the smooth Texas lilt caused every cell in her body to awaken and feel alive.

"Right now, Miss Kingman, I could do whatever I wanted to you and there's nothing you could do to stop me." He tightened his arm around her waist. Not painfully, but just enough to demonstrate his strength.

She didn't need the lesson. She was already

extremely aware of the muscles that surrounded her. And everything else about Gage Reardon. The warmth of his breath against her ear. The rise and fall of his chest against her back. The bulge of his bicep pressing into her breast. The flex of his fingers on her waist. The feel of his hand against her mouth.

He shifted that hand and his calloused fingers brushed her lips. A flash of heat spiked through her. Heat she'd never felt before. Not even with Danny. Terror turned to panic. She needed to get away from this man. She needed to get away now.

When his grip on her mouth loosened, she bit down hard on his finger. He released her with a muffled oath just as her brother called out her name.

"Addie! Addie!" Wolfe came running through the opening in the hedge. He stopped short when he saw them and heaved a relieved breath. "There you are. I thought you'd left the reception alone. I didn't know you were with Gage."

All Adeline had to do was tell her brother what Gage had done and he'd be fired on the spot. And probably beaten to a pulp as well. Her brothers might respect Gage and value his dedication and loyalty to the family, but they were extremely protective of her and her sister, Delaney. If Adeline told them Gage had gotten out of line, he'd be gone from the Kingman Ranch by morning. Adeline couldn't say she wouldn't be happy to see him go. She didn't know what had just happened, but she didn't want it to happen again.

And yet, she couldn't bring herself to tattle.

At least, not now.

Not when someone was out to get her family and had mutilated a bull, burned down the barn, assaulted a stable hand and her sister-in-law Lily, and tampered with the brakes on Stetson's truck, almost killing her and Stetson. Whoever it was had gotten more and more daring, and next time, someone could actually die.

The thought frightened Adeline. She couldn't lose anyone else. While she might not like the way Gage had manhandled her tonight, she knew he'd only done it to make her understand the danger she'd put herself in. Stetson trusted him to watch out for his family. That's exactly what Gage had been doing. His methods might've been extreme, but he hadn't actually hurt her. Now that he wasn't touching her, the feelings he'd evoked had receded back into their vault.

"As you can see, I'm fine, Wolfe," she said. "You don't have to be worried about me."

"Yes, you do." Gage ratted her out. "Your sister came out here alone. Something you would've known if you'd been doing your job of watching out for her—instead of chasing after all the single women at the reception."

She waited for Wolfe to set him straight. Her little brother might be a charmer with women, but he had a bad temper with men. Especially if they challenged him. But instead of bristling at Gage's reprimand, Wolfe laughed.

"Do you ever take a break, Gage? Okay, so I fell down on my job. You should try it some time. I heard Wally Rondo's daughter is interested in you. You can't tell me you wouldn't like to spend some time alone with that cute little farmer's daughter."

"I'm working tonight."

"You're always working. You and my brother are two peas in a pod." Wolf grinned. "But even Stetson stopped working long enough to find himself a woman. Go ask Miley Rondo to dance, Gage. You've certainly earned some time off. I won't tell Stetson and I'll take over keeping an eye on Adeline."

"I don't dance," Gage said.

Wolfe shrugged. "Suit yourself. But if you don't want to have fun, you shouldn't mind if I have some."

"It's not my job to take—" Before Gage could finish, Wolfe disappeared through the opening in the hedge.

Since Adeline wanted to be stuck with Gage as much as he wanted to be stuck with her, she quickly followed her brother. As a kid, she had played often in the labyrinth so she had no trouble finding her way out. Gage didn't make a sound, but she knew he followed close behind her. As she started to climb the stone steps that led to the garden where the reception was being held, he stopped her.

"Please don't leave the reception alone again."

It was still an order, but at least, this time, he'd said please. She turned and found him standing at the bottom of the steps. He looked up at her, and the lights strung throughout the garden fell across his face. He wasn't what you would call a handsome man. His features were all harsh angles: Square chin with a cleft. Pronounced jaw that was always covered in golden stubble. Wide mouth that rarely smiled—at least not at her. A nose that sat at an odd angle as if it had been broken and not properly set. Sharp cheekbones. Deep-set eyes. Broad forehead.

His only soft features were his eyes. They were hazel—more gold than green—and surrounded by long, lush lashes that any woman would envy. They stared back at her, waiting for some kind of confirmation.

"I won't leave the reception," she said.

He studied her for a long moment before he nodded. "Then goodnight, Miss Kingman."

He turned and disappeared into the darkness.

Leaving her alone once again.

Order on Amazon now:
*https://tinyurl.com/yuxft6hf*

# Other Titles by Katie Lane

Be sure to check out all of Katie Lane's novels!
*www.katielanebooks.com*

## Kingman Ranch Series
*Charming a Texas Beast*
*Charming a Knight in Cowboy Boots (April 2022)*
*Charming a Big Bad Texan (May 2022)*

## Bad Boy Ranch Series:
*Taming a Texas Bad Boy*
*Taming a Texas Rebel*
*Taming a Texas Charmer*
*Taming a Texas Heartbreaker*
*Taming a Texas Devil*
*Taming a Texas Rascal*
*Taming a Texas Tease*
*Taming a Texas Christmas Cowboy*

## Brides of Bliss Texas Series:
*Spring Texas Bride*
*Summer Texas Bride*
*Autumn Texas Bride*
*Christmas Texas Bride*

## Tender Heart Texas Series:
*Falling for Tender Heart*

# ABOUT THE AUTHOR

KATIE LANE IS A FIRM believer that love conquers all and laughter is the best medicine. Which is why you'll find plenty of humor and happily-ever-afters in her contemporary and western contemporary romance novels. A USA Today Bestselling Author, she has written numerous series, including *Deep in the Heart of Texas, Hunk for the Holidays, Overnight Billionaires, Tender Heart Texas, The Brides of Bliss Texas, Bad Boy Ranch,* and *Kingman Ranch.* Katie lives in Albuquerque, New Mexico, and when she's not writing, she enjoys reading, eating chocolate (dark, please), and snuggling with her high school sweetheart and Cairn Terrier, Roo.

For more on her writing life or just to chat, check out Katie here:
Facebook *www.facebook.com/katielaneauthor*
Instagram *www.instagram.com/katielanebooks*

And for information on upcoming releases and great giveaways, be sure to sign up for her mailing list at *www.katielanebooks.com*!

Printed in Great Britain
by Amazon